The Lawman's Surprise Family

Patricia Johns

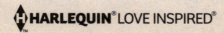

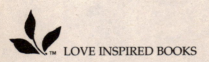

LOVE INSPIRED BOOKS

Recycling programs for this product may not exist in your area.

ISBN-13: 978-0-373-81898-3

The Lawman's Surprise Family

Copyright © 2016 by Patty Froese Ntihemuka

www.Harlequin.com

Printed in U.S.A.

"I'm willing to have you get to know our son," Sofia said.

"But I don't want to include anyone else in that right now," she continued. "Meeting his dad is big enough without complicating that. And that includes your family."

"So your whole family kept the secret?" he asked, a tinge of bitterness in his voice.

They had, and saying it out loud made it sound worse somehow. They'd all agreed that keeping the secret would be best for the child.

"Ben, I've been the center of Jack's world for his entire life," she said, her voice quivering with emotion. "This isn't about our families. Not yet, at least."

"Agreed," he said. "This should be about you and me."

Just about the two of them…well, the three of them now.

"We tried that once," she said past a lump in her throat. "It didn't work too well."

"Yeah." His voice was low and deep, and she suddenly wished she could lean into his strong shoulder, smell that old scent of leather and cologne and feel loved again. "Anyway, I'll see you tomorrow."

"Tomorrow," she repeated. *And for the next two weeks*, she thought.

Patricia Johns writes from northern Alberta where she lives with her husband and son. The winters are long, cold and perfectly suited to novel-writing. She has her BA in English lit, and you can find her books in Harlequin's Love Inspired and American Romance lines.

Books by Patricia Johns

Love Inspired

His Unexpected Family
The Rancher's City Girl
A Firefighter's Promise
The Lawman's Surprise Family

A person may think their own ways are right,
but the Lord weighs the heart.
—*Proverbs* 21:2

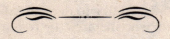

I'd like to dedicate this novel to my father,
a surprising fount of romance novel ideas.
Whenever I get stuck in a plot,
he can see the way out. Thank you, Dad!

And, of course, I'd like to dedicate this book to
my husband, who inspires the romantic in me.

I could never do what I do without the
love of these two sweet, supportive men.

Chapter One

The chances of avoiding Benjamin Blake in a town this size weren't in her favor, but it didn't stop Sofia McCray from hoping. If she could just get through today, she might be able to escape him until she was ready.

As she knocked on the police chief's office door, Sofia could make out the muffled voices of two men inside. After a moment, the door swung open to reveal a man with blond hair that was gray around the temples, an easy smile and a wedding ring. The Chief of Police badge shone on his blue uniform. He shook her hand and gestured her in.

"Good morning," Chief Taylor said. "Miss McCray, I presume?"

"Yes, from the *Haggerston Chronicle*," Sofia replied with a quick smile, mentally preparing herself for her assignment. She'd only started at the *Chronicle* a couple of weeks ago after returning to Haggerston, and this assignment meant that her editor was taking her seriously— for now. She wanted to keep it that way.

"Let me introduce you to the officer you'll be riding along with." He gestured to the chair in front of the large desk.

A tall officer, dark and rugged, sat with his arms crossed over his broad chest. His dark hair was cropped short, his blue uniform setting off his obsidian eyes. He cocked his head to one side as her gaze lit on him, and a small smile turned up one corner of his mouth. Her heart thumped hard and then seemed to stop in her chest. He needed no introduction—this was Benjamin Blake.

"You're late," Ben said, glancing at his watch. "Eight oh five."

She'd heard that he'd become a cop, but she'd had a hard time imagining her high school "bad boy" boyfriend in law enforcement. Looking at him in full uniform, his dark eyes fixed on her almost teasingly, she found herself tongue-tied.

She had some explaining to do, and she wasn't looking forward to it.

"Officer Blake says that he knows you already," Chief Taylor said. "So that should make working together for the next two weeks easier. We appreciate you being here, Miss McCray. Our new community watch program could use the publicity."

She finally found her voice. "Yes, absolutely."

"I just need you to sign a few papers." Chief Taylor passed her a clipboard with forms attached. Sofia took it numbly.

"Couple of days, I thought," Ben said to the police chief, and she glanced up from the papers.

"Or so…" the chief replied noncommittally. She didn't miss the tension that rippled along Ben's jawline and realized he wasn't looking forward to this, either.

She scratched her signature across the bottom line, and when the police chief flipped to the next page, she did the same once more. Sofia attempted to keep her expression neutral, her eyes moving over the forms without absorbing any of the information.

"In case you get shot," Ben offered helpfully, nodding at the forms. Humor flickered at the corners of his lips, and for a split second, she saw the teenager in him again. His gaze held hers for longer than necessary, and her breath caught in her throat. She forced her eyes back down to the page, heat rising in her cheeks.

"Just accepting that a ride-along has risks," the chief said cheerfully. "And that you won't sue us if anything should happen." He took the clipboard from her and turned away. "Officer Blake is one of the leading officers in this program. We're focusing on domestic violence, child endangerment and driving under the influence. We have bigger problems here in Haggerston than most people realize."

"Yes, I was briefed on that," she said. "I'm glad to be a part of getting the word out."

"Do you have any questions before you leave?" Chief Taylor asked.

"Not at the moment," she admitted. She was still too distracted by Ben's unexpected presence to think of much else.

"Well, I'm sure Officer Blake can fill you in when questions arise," he said with a smile as he turned away. "Have a good day, you two."

Ben pushed himself up from the chair where he'd been reclining and gestured for her to leave the office ahead of him. The door closed behind them, the din of the bull pen enveloping her. Sofia looked up at Ben, noting the subtle way his face had changed over the years. He had lines around his eyes now. His jaw was clean shaven—a change from the constant five o'clock shadow he used to sport. He still had those piercing dark eyes with long lashes, but he'd lost that familiar scent of leather jacket and cheap cologne. He was a man now, his teen years left solidly behind him. He seemed to sense her scrutiny, because he glanced down at her.

"It's been a long time," he said, his tone low enough for her ears alone as they made their way around the desks and toward the front door.

"Yes. Nine years." Nine years was a long time

to carry a secret. She'd come back to Haggerston knowing that she'd have to reveal it sooner or later, but it wasn't going to be easy.

"Something like that." He nodded at another officer, and she felt the warmth of his hand touch the small of her back as he guided her past some desks. "How long have you been back in town?"

"Two weeks." They emerged past the front desk and pushed open the front door, stepping out into the cool spring air.

"So, what brought you back after all this time?" Ben asked.

She wished she had a flippant reply for that question, but she didn't. She felt her smile fade.

"My dad has cancer," she said, her voice low. "I'm here to help him through his treatment."

That was an understatement. She was also here to try and rebuild a relationship with her father after all these years. When her parents split up that summer that she graduated, she'd done what all the counselors advised against— she'd chosen sides. Now that her father was facing cancer, she knew that she had a lot to make up for to him, as well. He'd met his grandson for the first time two weeks ago, and she truly wished she hadn't left it so long. This homecoming wasn't a victorious one by any stretch.

"I'm sorry, I had no idea." He reached toward her, but just before touching her arm, he pulled back.

"It's okay. We aren't really advertising it. Dad doesn't want anyone to treat him like he's sick." She touched the tingling place on her arm where he'd nearly touched her.

Ben nodded slowly. "I get that."

This was not going to be easy working with Ben. She'd thought she'd put all those butterflies behind her. She was a grown woman with responsibilities, for crying out loud, and she was smarter this time. Wiser. Older. Why couldn't that be enough? She stopped and turned around to face him. "Are you sure this is a good idea?"

"What, us working together?" he asked.

"Exactly. We have a bit of a history—"

"I tried getting out of it," he interrupted. "It was no use."

"Oh." He'd tried getting out of it? Somehow, she thought she'd be the one with more reservations, but perhaps she was wrong about that. Benji had been her first love—the bad boy with the motorcycle who swept her off her feet, much to her parents' chagrin. And she'd loved him passionately until he dumped her and she left town with her mother—pregnant. She'd never told him about her pregnancy or her plans to leave, and while the guilt of that laid heavily on her shoulders, she'd honestly thought she was doing him a favor.

"I know this is complicated..." she began.

"Yeah, a bit."

He angled his steps toward the parking lot, and she had to quicken her pace to keep up. Was he actually annoyed with her? It hardly seemed as though he had any right. She'd been the one unceremoniously dumped on the night of her prom. They'd been just about to go inside when she'd asked him the question that had been plaguing her for weeks: How would they stay together when she went off to college? It was a reasonable question, considering that Benji hadn't finished all the classes he needed to graduate that year, so he'd be staying behind. Somehow, that had turned into an argument that ended with Benji telling her that they'd never last anyway, and he'd driven off on his motorcycle, leaving her in the parking lot with a corsage and a broken heart.

"It looks like things have turned out well for you," she said, giving him an uncertain smile. "You look good."

It seemed like the polite thing to say, although what the social etiquette was in a situation like this, she had no idea.

"So do you," he said, ambling toward the row of squad cars. "Mind if I ask you something, now that I've got the chance?"

"Not at all." Again, that seemed to be the polite response, even though she wasn't exactly keen to face his questions.

"So how come you just disappeared like

that?" He glanced down at her, his gaze fixed on hers for a moment longer than necessary, then he nodded toward a cruiser. "This one is mine, by the way."

Little did he know that the least of her sins was the disappearing act, but if she had to be honest, she'd disappeared because she was afraid to face reality. And he had no idea how much reality had been hanging in that balance.

"It was a complicated time," she said hesitantly. "My parents had just told me that they were getting a divorce. They'd been fighting constantly for months. Then, when my mom said she was moving out, I—"

Her world had crumbled. She'd felt adrift— seventeen, alone, pregnant and without the stability of her parents' marriage to buoy her up. She could still remember how she'd begged them to reconsider, to go for therapy, to do anything to keep them together. They hadn't, obviously, and their breakup had decimated her.

"So, what happened, exactly?" Ben asked. "There were rumors about your parents and why your mom left."

"What kinds of rumors?" she asked, irritation rising. Her father had stayed in Haggerston, and the town should have known what kind of husband and father he'd been—not exemplary.

Ben unlocked her door and she got in. A moment later, he got into the driver's side and, without looking at her, said, "People said she met someone else."

"She wasn't cheating on my father," Sofia said dryly. "She'd just had enough. Sometimes women reach their limit."

"But you both left without saying goodbye to anyone," he said, finally looking in her direction. "I found out when I came by your place, and your dad told me you were gone. You never did answer my emails."

"We were broken up, if you recall," she said defensively. "I didn't just leave town without telling my boyfriend. I left without telling my ex-boyfriend. I was no longer your business."

"Technically," he replied evenly.

"What does that even mean?" she demanded. "We were seventeen. We were kids. Do you honestly think I owed you something after you broke my heart?"

She felt the hypocrisy of the words as they passed her lips. She'd left pregnant with his son—of course she owed him something! But he didn't know that, and his argument right now was surrounding the fact that she'd left at all without telling him her plans. And while she knew that she had to tell Ben about his son— and her son about his father—she'd wanted to wait until the time was right, until she had full control of the situation. Now that she was working with Ben, she'd have to tell him sooner than she'd planned, and her stomach sank at the thought.

"Yeah, I think you did owe me something," he said, and the heaviness in his tone made her wonder if perhaps he did know more than he was letting on. "We weren't just a couple, we were—"

She waited, but he didn't finish the sentence.

"We were each other's first loves," she concluded. "Even if that relationship was over—"

"I still loved you. That hadn't ended for me."

Sofia froze, his words tickling something deep inside of her. He met her gaze, held it, then put the key into the ignition and the cruiser rumbled to life. So if he'd still loved her, why dump her? Why leave her alone in the parking lot of the community center in a tulle gown? That didn't sound like love to her; though something in his voice suggested that he still felt something for her, and she couldn't help the heat that rose in her cheeks.

"Anyway," he said, breaking the silence. "Like I said, it's been a long time."

Her cell phone rang, and Sofia glanced down to see her father's number. It was a welcome interruption right then, and she picked it up before it could ring twice.

"Hi, Dad," she said, trying to keep her voice casual.

"Hi, kiddo," he said, using the same endearment he'd used as long as she could remember. "We, uh, have a situation over here."

"What kind of situation?" she asked.

"Jack is sick."

"Sick? How sick? Does he have a fever?"

"I don't know. He's throwing up, though, and it's not stopping."

She sighed. "Did you give him the gluten-free cereal for breakfast?"

"Of course."

"With the almond milk, not the dairy?"

"Uh, yeah. I think."

She closed her eyes. "What else did he have, Dad?"

"A cannoli."

"A cannoli? You gave him a cannoli?" she demanded. "That's full of everything he's allergic to!"

"I thought he was like other kids. They've got the metabolism of rats."

"Well, he's not," she replied, attempting to keep her anger in check. She'd explained all of this to her father in detail this morning. He'd said he understood. But this was like her father had always been, doing it his own way. What did he think, that she'd just been being dramatic when she explained all of this?

"What do I do?" He sounded contrite.

"I'm coming home," she said, and without

even saying goodbye, she punched the end button. Sofia glanced up to find Ben watching her, an odd expression on his face. When she looked over, he flicked his gaze back to the road ahead of him.

"You're a mom?" he asked after a moment.

"I am. I have a son—Jack."

"Everything okay over there?" he asked.

"Not really. Look, I know this is an inconvenience, but could we swing by my father's house so I can check on my son? He has allergies, and my father—" She shook her head. "I just need to make sure he's okay."

"Sure." He signaled a turn, and they headed back toward the main drag.

Sofia's mind was on Jack right then, his poor little digestive system in knots because of his grandfather's negligence. And because Jack didn't seem to take his own allergies as seriously as he should, either, if she had to be completely fair.

She glanced at Ben. She'd have to tell him soon—she knew that. But not yet. She had this under control, and when Ben knew that he was a father, everything would change. Working together would be more tense than it already was, and she'd have no escape. She couldn't afford to lose this precarious balance just yet.

"Thanks," she said with a smile. "I appreciate it."

* * *

She has a son. That little fact seemed to hit Ben in the gut like a sucker punch. He didn't know why it hadn't occurred to him before that she'd have children. In the time since high school, he'd gotten married and had a child, too.

He swallowed against the tightness in his throat.

He'd married Lisa four years ago. They'd met in a coffee shop when her car wouldn't start. He'd given her a jump from his cruiser and gotten her number. Six months later, they were married. Lisa had always wanted a baby, and they'd tried for two years before she finally got pregnant. It was supposed to be free sailing after that, and neither of them had expected the complications. Before she'd even had her first baby shower, Lisa was admitted to the hospital for high blood pressure. The baby was born via emergency C-section at six months, and his wife had died on the operating table. His baby girl died two days later in the NICU. At barely two pounds, she was too tiny to make it.

And Sofia had a son.

Was this jealousy he felt? Mandy was frozen at the newborn stage in his mind, but from time to time he wondered what little Mandy would be doing if she'd lived. Right now, she'd be a year and a half. She'd probably be toddling around and calling him Dada.

His daughter had been the reason why he wanted to clean up this town. When he'd found out his wife was pregnant, he'd gotten this sudden protectiveness at the very idea of this little person. He wanted Haggerston to be the kind of place a kid could grow up safe and happy. His own upbringing had been neither. When he'd lost his daughter, his drive hadn't changed. There were other kids growing up here—kids growing up just as poor as he had—and he wanted to make a difference for them, too.

"So how old is your son?" he asked.

"Eight."

He glanced over at her, frowning slightly. "Eight?"

She nodded. "Yes. He's in the third grade this year. And he's a smart kid. He started reading really early. And he loves jokes—they drive me nuts…"

"Jokes, huh?" he said absently.

She'd said the boy was eight. She'd been gone nine years… The mental math wasn't rocket science. Had she met someone right after him? That was a possibility. Sofia, with her almond skin and smooth, dark waves—she wouldn't have trouble finding someone else. He'd never tried to deceive himself in that area. He hadn't seen her in nine years, had a rocky history with her and had good reason not to trust her again, and he still found himself feeling things he didn't want to feel when looking at her. Imagine some poor guy who didn't have his defenses up—he'd never have a chance.

"Kid jokes." She shrugged. "He's a regular little comedian. Like, what do you call a flying police officer?"

Ben looked over at her mutely.

"A heli-copper," she concluded, giving him a wan smile.

Ben cracked a grin and shook his head. "Okay. Cute."

They were coming up on her father's street. It felt weird to be driving her back there, almost like the old days when he could feel her arms tightening around his middle as he took the turn around the corner. He could still remember the creak of his leather jacket as she held on tight, and the sound of her voice coming from behind, mingling with the growl of his motorcycle's engine.

Except they weren't seventeen now, and she was a mom. That changed a lot of things in his head, somehow. Time had passed, and there was no pretending otherwise.

"Thank you for this," she said as he slowed to a stop in front of the familiar old house. Her cell phone rang again, and she picked up the call as she got out. "Dad? Look, I'm here. Is he still throwing up?"

Ben got out, too. She hadn't exactly said that

she wanted privacy for this, and he found himself more than a little curious about her son. What was she like as a mother? So far, he could see the matter-of-fact side of her coming out, all concerned with vomiting and allergies. He'd probably be the same way if things had turned out differently. Lisa would have been the same way, too, although she'd never had the chance to even see her daughter—

He pushed the unbidden thoughts back and picked up his pace. He caught up with her at the side door and stepped inside after her. It had been a while since he'd been in Steve McCray's house. When Steve's wife had left him, he'd been a wreck and spent way too much time in bars. Ben had personally escorted Mr. McCray home again several times, and he'd always been struck by how different the old house looked with the women gone. It had gone from a somewhat cluttered but homey little place to a dank and dismal hole seemingly overnight.

The side door led into the kitchen, and when he glanced around he could already see Sofia's touch around the place. A vase of daisies— Sofia's favorite flowers—sat on the counter next to a stack of library books that looked to be a mixture of kids' books and murder mysteries. She'd always liked a good who-done-it. The kitchen table had an assortment of boxed foods, all of which had "gluten-free" written in big letters on them in some prominent place. The box of cannolis sat open beside the gluten-free fare, like the forbidden tree in the garden.

"Hi, Sofia—" Steve McCray stopped when he saw Ben. He nodded in Ben's direction.

Ben nodded his hello in return.

"Where is he?" Sofia asked, putting her hands on her hips and looking up at her father. Her eyes flashed dangerously, and Steve looked smart enough to take the warning.

"In the bathroom."

Sofia marched out of the kitchen without a backward glance, and Ben met Steve's gaze with a wan smile.

"So…" Steve said. "How're things with you?"

"Not bad." Ben shrugged. "Hanging in there."

Steve regarded Ben in a tense silence, then gestured to the box on the table. "Cannoli?"

"Don't mind if I do."

Each man took a cannoli and bit into the sweet, creamy centers. They chewed silently, the sound of Sofia's voice filtering through the walls while she talked with her son. She sounded gentle and sympathetic, although her words were too muffled to make out. A moment later, she came back into the room.

"He's done vomiting now," she said. "For the next couple of days he'll be still feeling pretty sick, though."

"Where is he?" Steve asked.

"Changing his shirt." She sighed, then glared at them in exasperation. "Are you two eating cannolis?"

Ben licked his fingers and shot Steve a guilty look. He had a feeling the two of them were going to step wrong no matter what.

"Just getting them out of the way so Jack doesn't need to even see them," Steve replied, and Sofia looked as if it was taking effort to bite her tongue. Coming with her into the house had been an obvious mistake.

"So are you taking the day off, then?" Ben asked her, edging toward the door. "This looks like family business…"

Sofia regarded Ben for a moment, then turned to her father.

"Dad, are you okay to look after him while I'm at work?" she asked. "He won't be much trouble feeling as badly as he does."

"Sure. We'll hang out," Steve replied. "I'm sorry about that. If I'd known what would happen—"

"I told you about his allergies!" she retorted, then sucked in a breath. "Okay, apology accepted. Just follow my instructions for his food from now on."

"Scout's honor." Steve shot her a grin, and before Sofia could react, a boy came padding into the kitchen.

"Mom?" He had a mop of dark hair and big

brown eyes that looked an awful lot like his mother's. He looked pretty tall for eight, but what did Ben know about these things? The boy paused when he saw Ben. "Hi," he said shyly.

"Hi," Ben said.

"Jack, this is one of my old friends, Ben," she said. "I'll be working with him for a little while."

"Oh." Jack's lips were on the pale side. He obviously wasn't feeling great. "Do I have to go to school today?"

"No, you can stay home," she said. "I'll call the school and tell them you're sick."

"Okay." Jack paused again. "I've got a new joke."

Sofia smiled and glanced toward Ben. "I told you he loves jokes, right? Okay, Jack. Let's hear it."

"What do you call cheese that isn't yours?" Jack asked, his gaze flickering toward Ben momentarily.

"Pretty much all of it, with your allergies," Sofia shot back.

"Nope. It's nacho cheese."

Ben laughed in spite of himself and shook his head. The kid was funny.

"So, can I watch TV?" Jack asked, turning his attention to his mother.

A smile twitched Sofia's lips, and he caught the humor that passed between mother and son. Jack was obviously pushing for something here.

"Only because you're sick and I feel sorry for Grandpa a little bit. As soon as you're better, the regular TV deal stands."

"Okay." Jack smiled. He still looked rather pale.

"Come here." She wrapped her arms around him and kissed the top of his head. "I love you, sweetie. I'm going back to work now. Call me if you need me, okay?"

Jack hugged her back. "Okay. Bye." When she released him, he headed into the living room, and the TV turned on.

"Feeling a little tired, myself," Steve said, glancing between Sofia and Ben. "I'll see you later."

Steve headed in the direction his grandson had gone, and on his way out, Ben noted that the older man looked thinner than he remembered. It was a small relief to be left alone with Sofia in the kitchen.

"You're all strict about TV watching, huh?" Ben said with a small smile.

"Afraid so." She caught his eye and shrugged. "I'm a far cry from the girl on the back of your motorbike, you know."

"I know." He pushed himself to his feet. "I'm a far cry from being the guy on the bike, too."

"Let me call the school, then we can get going." She sighed and shook her head. "Might as well get to work."

A couple of minutes later, they were both in the car, and Ben's mind was whirling. There was something about Jack…something he couldn't quite put his finger on. He looked like a good kid, and he looked an awful lot like his mother, but the timing was still nagging at him. Was it rude to ask if there was a chance that he was Jack's father? She would have told him if he'd gotten her pregnant, wouldn't she?

"Should I even ask this?" he asked, glancing at her uncertainly.

"Probably not," she joked.

"I'm being serious." He put the car into gear and pulled away from the curb. "He's eight. You left nine years ago. The timing is…" He trailed off, not finishing.

This was her cue to tell him that no, he was not Jack's father. This was the place where she was supposed to tell him the story of the guy who came after him. This was the place where he would laugh it off and say something like, "Just making sure!" The silence stretched out, and he glanced toward her uncertainly.

"Sofia?"

She sighed. "I meant to tell you in a better way."

Ben blinked, tightening his grip on the steering wheel. This wasn't the reply he actually expected.

"You want to make that a little clearer?" he asked.

"I—" Sofia sucked in a breath. "I wanted to tell you in a different way, but, yes, you're Jack's dad."

Silence fell between them, and the rumble of the motor seemed to grow louder by the second. Ben glanced at her a couple of times, then finally broke the silence.

"So—" His grip tightened on the steering wheel. "Wait, so he *is* mine?"

He pulled a hand through his hair, trying to sort out exactly what he felt, but there was nothing there right now but shock.

"Yes, Benji," she said after a moment. "Jack is most certainly yours."

Chapter Two

Ben rubbed a hand over his forehead, Sofia's words sinking in. Jack…was his? He was a dad again? Not really again, exactly. More like he'd been one all along and never been let in on that little detail. This felt more like a bad dream—things coming at him faster than he could entirely make sense of them.

When she used his old nickname—Benji—it reminded him of all those feelings they used to share, and something inside of him suddenly rebelled, and he felt a flood of anger.

It was a feeling, at least. Something besides shock, but the uppermost thought in his mind was, *This isn't fair to Lisa and Mandy*. It felt like betraying them after the fact, and it stabbed hard.

"Ben," he said gruffly.

"Pardon me?" Her voice sounded weak, and when he glanced in her direction, he found her wan and pale, big dark eyes fixed on him uncertainly.

"I don't go by Benji anymore. I'm Ben."

It was a small complaint in the grand scheme of things, but hearing his old nickname grated at him something fierce. She'd always called him Benji, and he used to love it, but when he'd met his wife and she'd also tried to call him Benji, he'd put a stop to it. Lisa had deserved something unique—something that hadn't been done before. Lisa had deserved to be the first for something. He'd always felt slightly guilty for not being able to completely forget about Sofia, and now that Lisa had passed away, the guilt was compounded. He hadn't given his wife the wholehearted devotion that she deserved.

That wasn't the point here, though, and he brought his mind back to the petite brunette beside him. Sofia sat in silence, seemingly willing to let him digest what she'd just told him.

"So how?" he asked, turning into a parking lot and choosing a spot as far from the other cars as possible. He slammed the car into Park. There was no way he could have this conversation while driving. "I don't get it. You were pregnant when you left? Did you know?"

"I knew." She nodded, and two pink circles materialized on her cheeks. "I was only a few weeks along, and we'd just broken up."

"It isn't like we hadn't broken up and gotten back together before," he said.

"I didn't want to get back together. The baby made everything different."

"Different." He heard the bitterness in his own voice. He wasn't sure why he was spoiling for a fight right now, but he was angry—deeply angry. This was a big load to dump on a guy, and why on earth had she waited so long to tell him?

"I should have told you sooner, I know," she said, as if reading his mind. "At first, I admit that I wasn't going to tell you anything, but deep down I knew that was wrong. And the older Jack got, the more curious he got. Other kids had dads, and I knew I had to tell you that he existed, but when I got as far as picking up the phone, I didn't have the words."

"How about, 'You've got a son'?" he suggested, his tone sarcastic. "That might have been a good start."

"I didn't even know if you'd care!"

"If I'd care?" he shot back, the insult slipping deep beneath his defenses. "Of course, I'd care!"

She actually wondered if he'd care that he'd fathered a child? Was that how low her opinion was of him? Did she think that he wouldn't have cared about her in all of this, either? He'd never have left her to have a baby on her own... He'd have found some way to take care of her.

"You care now!" Her eyes snapped in anger.

"You weren't like this before! You were…" She shook her head irritably. "You were the guy with the leather jacket and the motorcycle. You hated authority. You were seventeen, you just about got expelled from school, and you were—"

"The father," he interrupted. "I was the father. I deserved to know."

He had changed. He had to admit that, if only to himself. He'd changed when he found God, and then he'd changed even further when he found Lisa. Lisa had tamed him in a whole different way, introducing him to matching linens and Sunday brunches.

"What would you have done?" she asked. "You weren't old enough to be a dad."

"You weren't old enough to be a mom." He turned his attention out the window for a moment, trying to wrap his mind around all of this. The facts seemed to float on the surface of his mind without actually penetrating deeply enough to feel real.

"I'll give you that." Her tone softened. "It wasn't easy."

"So why?" he pressed. "Why not tell me later? Why not call me after he was born?"

"I was trying to protect him." She said it so matter-of-factly, as if it were the most natural answer in the world.

"From me?" he asked, incredulously. Her silence seemed to confirm it, and he shook his head. "What did you think I was going to do? Did you really think I was that much of a jerk?"

"I didn't think you'd want to be in his life," she said.

"So you didn't bother giving me the chance?"

"You weren't exactly father material!"

There it was. The truth stung. He'd been a messed-up kid, looking for trouble. He'd flouted authority, put all of his money into his motorbike and taken great pride in doing things his own way. But he'd been a teenager, so it wasn't surprising that he hadn't been acting like an adult yet.

"I've grown up," he said quietly. "Was I really so bad?"

"There was a lot going on at the time," she admitted, and she pulled her dark hair away from her face. "My mom used to warn me about rebel boyfriends. My dad had been hers—did you know that? You were just like him—making your own rules, the rebel without a cause. But that doesn't translate well into parenthood. It's hard having a father like mine."

Ben remembered Sofia's strained relationship with her father. He'd often wondered if she'd jumped onto the back of his bike so readily just to see if her dad would try to stop her. Her father never had—not in the obvious ways, at least. Ben had never had a father in his life, either, so he'd never been one to judge someone else's daddy issues—something his own son would probably have plenty of, too.

"I know this is a lot to dump on you at once." Sofia broke the silence. "I don't know what else to say. I'm sorry. I was afraid. You have to understand it from my perspective. I was having a baby, and I loved that baby more than anything else in the world, even when he was too tiny for me to even show—"

Did she think she had the monopoly on love? It wasn't all that different for fathers.

"I know exactly what that's like," he said.

"You do?" Sofia stopped, swallowed. "You have children?"

He hadn't meant to bring Lisa and Mandy up, and he heaved a sigh. Here Sofia was in the flesh, a reminder of how he'd failed his wife, bringing the news that they'd made a baby together back before he'd become a Christian—long before he'd met Lisa. And to make matters even worse, when he looked at Sofia McCray, he still saw that gorgeous girl who used to make his heart skip a beat. He wasn't about to tell her about the family he lost—not yet.

"Never mind. We have work to do," he replied gruffly. He restarted the car.

She was silent, and he was relieved when he saw a pickup truck whipping through a four-way stop and weaving from one lane to the other. He sent up a silent, and ironic, prayer of thanks for the distraction. He knew who this was—it was Mike Layton, a local journalist he'd already arrested three times for domestic violence.

"Hold on," he said, slapping on the siren and stepping on the gas. The cruiser roared forward, and Sofia was pushed back into her seat, her eyes widening in surprise.

Making sense of past pain was hard. Pulling over an intoxicated driver—that was his comfort zone. He'd enjoy this one a little bit, and if Mike had been drinking, there was no way he was letting him get home before a nice, lengthy detox. Mavis Layton's safety relied upon that.

The car lurched, and Sofia sucked in a breath of surprise, her stomach hovering in her middle as the car catapulted them forward. Ben's expression was steely, and he moved with precision, his hands sliding over the steering wheel with the fluidity of practice. This was a side to him she'd never seen before—the cop at work— and she found that she wasn't afraid with him behind the wheel. Nauseated from being whipped around, perhaps, but not afraid.

That had always been the allure of Benji Blake—his complete confidence in his own abilities. She remembered how her mother used to lecture her about riding on the back of his bike, but she'd never felt at risk while he was driving. There was something about the feel of his leather jacket in her grip, her helmet resting against his back as they sped along the familiar old roads. He'd gone too fast, and he'd kept her out too late, but he'd never made her feel unsafe. Not once. Except it was no motorcycle now, it was a police cruiser, but the feeling was uncomfortably similar.

The blue pickup truck ahead of them wove to the other side of the road, then slowed to a stop at the curb. She strained to get a better look.

"Is he drunk?" Sofia asked.

"That's my guess," Ben said, punching the plate number into the computer on his dash. "You can come out with me, but stand back."

He put a hand on the butt of his gun and reached for the door handle.

"Don't you need to wait to figure out who he is?" she asked, jutting her chin in the direction of the computer on the dash. A smile flickered at his lips.

"I know who he is. That's Mike Layton—one of the writers at your paper."

"That's Mike?" She shaded her eyes against the morning sunlight. Mike didn't seem like the type to have a drinking problem, not that she knew him very well, only having been at the job for a week. Landing this assignment was due to her experience in this kind of research with the last paper she'd worked for in California. She should be grateful for this assignment, but right now she found herself wishing that she'd been a little less ambitious when she arrived.

Ben got out of the car and headed toward the driver's side of the truck. Sofia unbuckled her seat belt and got out, edging closer so that she could hear their words, but still attempting to stay out of Mike's immediate line of sight. It would be awkward if her coworker knew that she saw him at his worst.

Ben pulled open the truck's door and stepped back.

"Step outside, Mike," Ben said, gesturing toward the side of the road. "Drinking this morning?"

"No," Mike retorted. "This is ridiculous. Don't you have better things to do than to harass me?"

"Step outside the vehicle." Ben's tone turned stony, and Mike reluctantly got out and muttered something under his breath.

"Hey, get your hands off me!" Mike snapped as Ben easily flipped Mike around so that his stomach was against the truck, and pulled out some cuffs from his belt. Ben was muscular and solid, the smaller man giving no contest.

"Hey, seriously!" Mike said loudly. "I didn't do anything!"

"Speeding, failure to stop at a stop sign, erratic control of the motor vehicle…" Ben seemed to be enjoying this, and he slapped the cuffs down on Mike's wrists a little harder than necessary. Mike winced as the metal tightened down with a series of clicks. "And some general disrespect to an officer of the law. Sit tight." Ben led Mike around the side of the truck. "We'll do a Breathalyzer."

"Are handcuffs really necessary?" the smaller man asked huffily, then his gaze fell on Sofia. Color suffused his face, and he looked away. Sofia pitied Mike in that moment, and anger rose up inside of her. Was Ben trying to prove something, or was he just taking out his anger about the revelations that morning? And how exactly was this kind of heavy-handed policing supposed to create the kind of environment where a community watch program was even effective?

Ben ambled past Mike and headed for the cruiser once more. He paused at Sofia's side, putting a gentle hand on her arm as he nudged her over so he could reach into the car.

"Excuse me, ma'am," he said, his voice low enough for her ears only. He grabbed the Breathalyzer packet and eased back out of the car again. "So, for your article, I should tell you that I've apprehended a suspected drunk driver. He was acting belligerently toward an officer and was subdued at the side of the road. I'm about to administer a Breathalyzer test to ascertain the extent of his sobriety."

His police jargon was over the top, and she glanced back at Mike, who wriggled uncomfortably in the cuffs.

"Is this about you and me?" she asked pointedly.

"Nope."

"So this is you being professional?" she asked, keeping her voice low.

"Sure is." He gave her a slow smile. "What's the problem?"

"Aren't you being a little rough with him?" she asked.

Obviously Ben didn't like Mike, but that was no excuse to abuse his position of authority—and that was exactly what this looked like. He also seemed a little too eager with those cuffs. Was this what happened when rebels chose the law as their cause—common bullying?

"Too rough? No, I don't think so," Ben replied, and ambled in Mike's direction without looking back.

"I'm not drunk," she heard Mike say. "I'm in a hurry. For crying out loud, Ben."

Ben didn't hurry his movements, and after a moment of fiddling, held the plastic straw from the Breathalyzer machine in front of Mike.

"Blow here."

Mike complied, and there was a moment while Ben looked down at the results. He glanced back at Sofia, disappointment in his expression.

"Not drunk, after all," Ben said with a sigh.

"Get me out of these cuffs!" Mike snapped. "I'm on the way to the hospital. My wife broke her wrist, and they asked me to meet her there."

Ben hooked a thumb over his belt and eyed Mike thoughtfully for a moment, then he glanced back in Sofia's direction.

"Uncuff him," she said, shaking her head. She knew she didn't really have a say in this, but she was angry nonetheless. Nothing infuriated her more than men with power who abused their positions—regardless of their reason.

Ben shrugged and pulled out the key to unlock the cuffs. Mike rubbed his wrists and glared in Ben's direction.

"You're an idiot, Ben!" Mike said.

"That's Officer Blake, to you," Ben said icily. "And I sincerely hope you were miles away when your wife got hurt."

Ben took a step forward, and Mike's attitude evaporated. He held up his hands.

"I was," Mike said. "Just let me go see if she's okay."

Obviously there was a history between these two, evident by their mutual dislike, but Ben had the upper hand here. He was in the position of authority, and he was leaning on it. He didn't seem any different from the Benji Blake she'd fallen in love with all those years ago—ever the rebel.

"Drive to the hospital slowly," Ben said, his voice low. "I'm watching you."

After they'd both gotten back into the car, Ben looked over at Sofia, then frowned when he noticed her expression.

"What?" he said.

"What was that?" she demanded. "I get that Mike is a bit of a jerk, but that doesn't mean you can push him around like that. There are laws against that sort of thing!"

"I have my reasons," Ben replied, starting the car again. He pulled out behind Mike's truck, following him down the road in the direction of the hospital.

"Care to share them?" she retorted. "Because that looked like a flagrant abuse of power. I'm frankly rather surprised that you'd do that to a journalist, especially with another journalist present to corroborate the story."

"Can't say too much legally," he replied. "And I can't take the chance of it going into one of your articles." He gestured in the direction of her tablet.

She sighed and turned the tablet upside down. If he had a reason, she'd like to hear it. "All right, you have my word that it's off the record."

Ben shrugged. "Let's just say Mike had it coming."

"So a personal vendetta?" she clarified.

He eyed her for a moment, then put his attention back on to the road. "You don't think too much of me, do you? No. I've personally arrested Mike Layton three times for beating up his wife."

Sofia froze. She hadn't seen that coming. Mike didn't seem like the type—loud, obnoxious and opinionated, yes, but violent? There was a picture of Mike's wife on his desk at the office, a slender woman with gentle eyes...

"And you thought—" she started.

"I thought that he was drunk," he replied with a shrug. "If I can stick him in the drunk tank instead of sending him home to Mavis, then I think that's a job well done. I really hope he was as far away from Mavis as possible when she broke her wrist, but I have to say, I have my doubts about that. Why she stays with him, I'll never know."

Sofia sighed and nodded. "I didn't know that about Mike."

She understood Ben's anger and his desire to make Mike uncomfortable, even for a little while, but that didn't cover everything for her.

"You're still playing by your own rules," she said. "You were like this when we were together—always doing everything your own way. Even if it would only hurt you in the end, you had to have it your way."

Ben glanced at her, then signaled a turn, still following Mike, as promised. "My way is effective." A twinkle of humor came into his eyes, and she shook her head.

"You cuffed a man without cause. That isn't even legal."

"I had cause," he retorted. "Just not…immediate. You're thinking of poor, mistreated Mike. What about Mavis? Mavis knows that all she has to do is mention my name, and her husband backs off. That's something positive, I'd say. And giving women a safe place to go and a number to call when their husbands get abusive is part of what we're trying to do with this community watch project. It's about the community looking out for each other and cops being called right away, not when it's too late. If the women don't trust us, all the programs in the world aren't going to make any difference."

She had to agree with the results, but she wasn't convinced of his methods.

"You've always done things your own way," she said after a moment. "And while I get it this time, it'll catch up with you eventually."

"You think I'm some kind of rogue cop, dealing out my own version of justice?" he asked, humor edging his tone.

"Yes." She had to admit that was exactly what she thought. He was the same old Benji Blake, except this version had a badge and a gun. As a teen, she'd found it exciting and alluring, but not now as an adult, and certainly not as a mother.

They were nearing the hospital, and Ben gave his siren one whoop of farewell, then eased past Mike's truck and kept on their way.

"Sofia, you don't have to worry about me," Ben said quietly. "I'm a decent guy."

She was silent, considering. Was he a decent guy, or was he just an older version of the same rebel he'd always been? If it weren't for her son in the mix, she wouldn't have cared so much, but Ben's character would have a huge impact on Jack. Jack would idealize Ben. He'd look up to him. He'd emulate him, and the last thing she needed was a son who turned out exactly like his father.

"Just keep in mind that I'm a journalist first," she said with a sigh. "I'm here to write articles that can help improve the public's perception about the police force, but I'm not going to lie, either. Don't put me in the position of having to write up a story that sets back your entire project."

Ben's jaw tightened. "I'll have you know that I care about this—more than you probably realize. You lived on the good side of the tracks, but I saw a different side to this town growing up. I'm going to fix that, whatever it takes. So you might have your ideals right now, but I've got more than ideals. I've got a plan, and I'm not afraid to put it into action."

Sofia didn't answer. Ben might be a cop, but

she was a journalist, and she had a responsibility to her job as well as to this town. The laws
were there for a reason, and she found it ironic
that she was now pushing against Benji from the
other side of the law. But Ben was like that—
rock solid, completely immoveable and always
perched right on the line. Some things would
never change.

Chapter Three

That evening, after dropping Sofia off at her father's house, Ben drove back to the other side of town where his mother lived. His mind was still chewing over the fact that he was a father, and he didn't know exactly how to process it all. He'd made plans to have dinner with his mother several days ago, and he didn't have the heart to break them. Besides, his mom deserved to know about this. A grandson would impact her life, too.

The trailer park was located on the east side of Haggerston, surrounded by a corrugated metal fence that corralled two looping roads, both lined by aging mobile homes. This had been home sweet home when Ben was being raised by his struggling single mother, Shyla Blake. She'd worked two jobs for as long as he could remember, and now that he could afford to pay her rent elsewhere, she downright refused to move.

"I'm fine," she'd said. "Just fix the heat and get me an air conditioner. It might be humble, but it's home."

Ben had to admit that it did feel like home still, in spite of it all. His mother's time had been monopolized by providing for him, and as a result, Ben had been generally unsupervised for much of his childhood. His mother worked the night shift at the front desk of a local hotel, and she'd call just to check on him. He could remember muting the TV to talk to her for a minute or two before she was noticed by her particularly grumpy boss. She'd done her very best for Ben, and whatever mistakes he'd made growing up certainly hadn't been her fault.

Ben got out of the squad car, locked the door and headed up the walk. His mother flung the door open before he even reached the steps. She was a short woman with mouse-brown hair— dyed to stay that way—that was pulled up in a high ponytail and hair sprayed to stay in a floofy '80s do that she couldn't be convinced to relinquish.

"Hi, honey. I was so glad you said you were coming for supper. Come on in."

The sound of a game show floated through the background, and he followed her inside, kicking the door shut behind him. His mother gave him a peck on the cheek, and he sank into one of two chairs that flanked a tiny, flyer-covered kitchen table.

"Macaroni and cheese?" he asked, nodding toward the stove.

"Your favorite," she said, turning down the TV volume. "You look tired."

"I'm wiped."

"So I heard from Ellen who heard from Liza at the deli that Sofia McCray is back in town," his mother said, shooting him an apologetic look. "Is it true?"

"Afraid so," he replied.

"I'm surprised she'd show her face around here," his mother muttered. "After she and that uppity mother of hers just walked off the way they did. Not a word to anyone—and left poor Steve by himself…"

She'd left Ben, too, for that matter.

"I always said Valentina McCray was hiding a bad core," his mother went on. "And Sofia is just like her mother. I always said it, didn't I? And you never believed me. I don't know what all Valentina was hiding—an affair? Maybe even mob connections—"

"Being Italian doesn't make her mafia," Ben said with a sigh.

"I know, I know…" His mother turned back to the stove, lifting the lid off the bubbling pot to release some steam. "I've always said that I don't care what country the girl is from, as long as she's got a good heart. I've always said that, haven't I? But the proof is in the pudding with that one!"

Ben wasn't sure if "that one" referred to Sofia or her mother, but it probably didn't much matter at this point of the conversation. His mother didn't care for either woman. Everyone had known that the McCray marriage hadn't been rock solid, but the gossips of Haggerston blamed it on Valentina because she was high-spirited, even though Steve hadn't seemed to complain. Valentina was petite with a dark complexion that made her look twenty years younger than she was—sparking the envy of every woman in town. When Valentina up and left her husband, that was proof enough about her "bad core" in his mother's books.

This was an old, oft-repeated conversation. They both knew it like the backs of their hands, and they went over it from time to time, just to buff it back to a shine. Ben's mother had been thrilled when Ben had broken up with Sofia, even if he'd only done it because her father had convinced him that he was a loser who would just hold her back. Sofia had graduated high school and earned scholarships for her high grades. Ben hadn't even graduated with his class that year, and he wouldn't be going anywhere. That had done a number on his confidence. Steve McCray had told him privately that it was only a matter of time before Sofia saw what a loser he was and she'd move on to someone worthy of her. It made sense, and when Sofia had started questioning him about the future there in the parking lot, it had all crumbled down around him. He couldn't offer her a future. He had nothing to give. So Ben had broken it off and driven away, convinced that if he did the dumping instead of getting the same treatment from her, it would be easier to bear. It hadn't been, and he'd spent the past nine years wishing he'd at least gotten a goodbye.

"I actually saw Sofia today," Ben said.

"Oh?"

"She's a journalist now—"

"Well la-di-da." Her voice dripped distain.

"And she's been assigned to ride along with an officer for a couple of weeks to cover this new community watch project we're starting up." He shot his mother a boyish grin. "And the officer she's riding with is me."

His mother regarded him in silence for a long moment. "You're kidding," she finally said.

Ben shook his head. "I'm dead serious."

"Don't you go falling for her again," his mother said. The pot started to boil over, and she whipped it off the burner.

Not falling for Sofia was easier said than done. Sitting with her in the car all day, the soft, floral scent of her wafting through the cab, had been awkward, but it had also been the sort of thing he'd dreamed about for the past nine years—another chance to just be next to her. He'd never really thought that he'd see her again.

"So what is she like now?" his mother asked as she tossed the noodles into a colander.

"She's—" How was he supposed to tell his mother this? He swallowed. "She had a bit of news for me."

She slowly raised her head, her brow crinkling in suspicion. "What kind of news?"

"She has an eight-year-old son." He met his mother's gaze and sucked in a breath. "And he's mine."

"Yours?" she asked weakly. "Are you sure? She could be lying."

"No, I'm pretty sure," he replied, shaking his head. "She didn't seem too thrilled about me being his father as it is."

Tears welled up in his mother's eyes, and she stood stock-still for a long moment.

"You have a son," she said in amazement. "That means I have a grandson."

"Yeah, that's how it works," he said.

Then she dabbed at her mascara with the heel of one hand. "After little Mandy..."

He didn't know what else to say, even though nothing else was necessary. His mother had been there with him through the whole ordeal when he lost Lisa and Mandy. She'd stood next to him like a soldier during the funeral, holding him up with the sheer force of her will and all of the muscle she had in her one-hundred-and-forty-pound body.

"Have you seen him?" his mother asked after a moment of silence.

"For about two minutes today. It was short."

"What's his name?"

"Jack."

"And Sofia—what does she want?" she asked warily.

"Nothing that I know of," he replied. "She just felt obliged to let me know, I guess."

"After nine years?" she snapped. "She waited nine whole years to let you know that you have a son, and you think she doesn't want anything? Mark my words, she wants money."

"If he's my son, I'll support him," Ben replied. "I have no problem with that."

"What about her—is she married?" his mother pressed.

"No, she's single, and before you start worrying, I don't think she has any interest in me. In fact, she seems to think I'm no better than I was at seventeen."

"You were a good kid." His mother frowned.

"I got into a lot of trouble, Mom."

"But you had a good heart," his mother argued. Hearts were weighed differently than behavior, in her estimation of things.

"Of gold." He could hear the bitterness in his own tone.

His mother had always believed that he was an innocent lamb, regardless of his suspension from school multiple times and a few serious warnings from the local police. Ben had been angry back then, and while he'd loved Sofia heart and soul, he wouldn't have made a good husband or father. He could see that, and the most painful part of all of this was that he couldn't entirely blame Sofia for making the choice that she did, even though that choice hurt him. A mother might love you no matter what you did, but a wife or a girlfriend—those were different rules to play by. And like Sofia had said, sometimes a woman just had a limit. Could he really blame her for drawing a line?

"At least Lisa didn't know about all of this," his mother said, her chin quivering at the memory, and he felt that old stab of guilt.

"No, Lisa should have known."

"Just to hurt her?" his mother countered. "I think, for her, not knowing was kinder."

"She could have made a more informed decision before marrying me," he muttered.

Lisa had known about Sofia before they got married, and in their first year of marriage she'd stumbled across an old love letter Sofia had written him. Lisa had been hurt, not that he blamed her. She'd wanted to know why he kept it still, and while she'd never made any demands, he knew what he should have done—thrown it away. But he couldn't. So he'd stashed it in the bottom of a drawer and felt uncomfortable all the same.

If an old letter could make Lisa feel territorial, what about a son? She'd gone through enough with him, and if she'd known that he and Sofia had a child together, she might not have thought that hitching her wagon to him was worth it. He certainly wouldn't have blamed her.

"Grab me the milk," his mother said, and Ben fetched the carton of milk from the fridge and passed it to her.

"He seems to have a lot of allergies," Ben said.

"Allergies?" She poured a slosh of milk into the pot. "That did *not* come from us. We Blakes may be a lot of things, but we're healthy as horses."

"Don't take it so personally. Allergies are common these days."

"He must look like you," his mother said, shooting him a smile. "Do you have a picture?"

"He looks like Sofia to me," he admitted. "He's got her dark hair and big, brown eyes. But no picture. Sorry."

His mother gave the pot of macaroni and cheese a brisk stir, then nodded toward the table. "Clear off the flyers, would you?"

Ben did as she asked, sweeping the whole lot of them into a cardboard box that sat by the table for that purpose.

"So, what took her so long to tell you?" she asked, then plunked the pot into the center of the table and turned her back on him to grab some plates.

"I don't know. I asked that, too. She said she was trying to protect him."

"From who?" his mother demanded, coming back with two Corningware plates in hand. "You? Me? What are we going to do but love that little boy?"

He didn't have any more answers than she did, and he heaved a tired sigh. "I don't think I ever met my dad's family, either."

"They didn't want to meet you," his mother replied. "But I do want to get to know Jack. I'm his grandma...granny. Nana?" She raised her eyebrows. "Do I look like a nana?"

Ben laughed in spite of himself. "That's a little premature."

"Eight years... That's not premature at all," she retorted.

Many a night, his mother had mixed up an over-boiled pot of macaroni and cheese for him, sat down across from him at this very table and listened to him talk about his day. To this day, nothing tasted better than an overcooked Kraft Dinner—not that they ever got the "good brand."

"So, what are you going to do?" she asked, pouring a puddle of macaroni into his plate and then passing him a fork. She settled herself across from him. "Do you know?"

"I'm going to try and get to know him," he replied. "I'm not going to let him grow up wondering if I cared."

She nodded. "Good."

"I just need to talk to Sofia and see if we can figure something out."

She nodded slowly, but she didn't say anything else. Ben imagined there wasn't much else to be said. There was a child, but Jack had a mother who stood between him and the rest of the world, and even Shyla Blake could respect that. She'd been a single mother, too, after all.

They both picked up their forks and started to eat. His mind wasn't on the food, though; it was on Sofia. He could still remember how it had felt when he'd gone to Sofia's house a couple of days after their breakup, just to find her father standing behind the screen door in his bathrobe, his face haggard and his body oozing the smell of alcohol.

"You're looking for Sofia?" he'd asked bitterly. "You're a day too late. She and her mother left."

"Left for where?" he'd demanded.

The older man had shrugged. "Don't know. Just left."

They'd stood there and stared at each other for a minute or two until the older man slowly shut the door, leaving Ben on the step, his heart suspended with shock. He'd dumped her and broken her heart, and she'd done what she had every right to do—left. She didn't need to stick around and deal with him any longer, but he'd still hoped that he'd have a chance to say he was sorry. Was it selfish? Probably. And now she was gone, without any warning and without so much as a goodbye.

After he'd left the McCray house nine years earlier, Ben had gone back home, and his mother had made him a pot of macaroni and cheese and held him while he cried. Ben's mother had loved him. Loved him like a rock. She'd seen the best in him when he failed to see it in himself, and every single time he sank into that kitchen chair, feeling like a failure and filled to the brim with anger at the world, she'd say the same thing.

"Benji," his mother said, her voice pulling him back to the present.

"Yeah, Ma?"

"You're a good man. And you're my son. You remember that, okay?"

"Okay, Ma."

That's what she'd said to him every night. *You're a good boy, Benji. And you're my boy. You remember that, okay?*

She'd loved him like a rock.

* * *

Sofia didn't believe in dieting. Having been raised by an Italian mother, she knew how to cook, and she knew how to eat, too. Her one concession was her nightly ritual on the treadmill, working off a few of the calories. And as for the few extra pounds she carried since high school, well, she embraced them along with the Italian cooking.

She was a little rounder now, a little softer, and a little stronger, too. Motherhood did that to a woman, and she had no complaints—that was a little piece of wisdom from her mother.

Wear some lipstick and clothes that fit. Where's the joy in life if you can't eat a full meal?

In fact, when Sofia had talked to her mother on the phone that evening, she'd said the same thing. Valentina believed in a woman's right to eat a full plate of food, and she reminded Sofia of that on a regular basis.

Sofia wiped her forehead with a towel, breathing hard as the base automatically inclined to make the workout hurt just a little bit more. Jack was in the tub, and her father was watching TV in his bedroom, leaving the downstairs to herself. Her favorite crime drama was playing, an episode she'd already seen, but it was a comforting routine—treadmill and TV. Her mind wasn't on the show, however. She needed to have a long overdue talk with Jack tonight, and she wasn't sure how she was going to do this.

Lord, give me the words. Let me do this properly...

She heard the plug pull upstairs, and the water started to drain. Jack would be down any minute, wanting his snack before bed, so she stopped the treadmill and gratefully got off. Her legs felt like jelly, and she wiped her face once more as she headed into the kitchen to dish up a bowl of applesauce for her son. It would be gentle on his stomach after the cannolis today.

A few minutes later, Jack ambled into the kitchen. His pajama shirt was done up one button off, and his fingers looked pruney from the tub. He slid into his spot at the table and pulled the bowl of applesauce closer. He took a tentative bite.

"I wanted to talk to you about something," Sofia said, sinking into the chair next to him. "Something really important."

"Did I do something bad?" Jack asked warily.

"No, sweetie." She reached over and put a hand on his arm. "Nothing bad, at all."

"Oh, that's good, then." He took another bite, his spoon clinking against the side of the bowl.

"You know how you've been asking about your dad?" she asked. He'd been asking more often over the past couple of years, and she'd been giving him as little information as possible, even though she knew it was the wrong choice. He needed answers.

Jack nodded but didn't say anything. His eating slowed, though, so she knew that she had his attention.

"Is there anything you'd like to ask about him now?" she asked hopefully.

Jack swallowed and frowned. "I *have* a dad, right?"

"Yes, you do," she said quietly. "I didn't tell him about you, though."

"Who is he?" Jack asked.

"You met him today. He's Benjamin Blake," she said, and then closed her mouth, waiting for the information to sink in.

"The policeman?"

"Yes, the police officer," she said.

"Does he know about me?" he asked after a moment.

"He didn't know about you when he was here this morning. I told him after we left."

"Was he happy to hear about me?"

That was a difficult question to answer. Her ride-along with Ben had not been smooth or comfortable. Ben was most certainly angry with her about not telling him earlier, and while fatherhood obviously hadn't been part of his plans right now, he'd been adamant that he did care about his son.

"Sweetie, you are very good news," she said gently. "You were a bit of a surprise, though."

"Hmm." Jack nodded slowly. "What's his name again?"

"Benjamin Blake."

"I'm a McCray," Jack said defensively. "I don't have to stop being a McCray, do I?"

"Of course not!" Sofia slipped an arm around him and pulled him against her. "You're always going to be my boy, Jack. That will never change, and you and I are McCrays. Period."

Jack was silent, and she couldn't see his face past his ruffled hair. What was he feeling? Was he going to be mad at her, too, for having waited so long?

"So..." Sofia paused and nudged him up so she could see her son's face. "How do you feel about this?"

"I don't know if I want a dad," Jack replied after a moment.

"How come?" she asked.

"I have you." Tears misted his eyes.

"Yes, you do." Sofia planted a kiss on the top of his head. "Look, Jack, you don't have to worry about anything. You aren't going to lose me. I'm your mom. That doesn't change. Okay?"

Jack nodded. "Does he have any kids? Do I have a brother or sister?"

"I don't think so, sweetie. I think you're the only one."

"Do I have another grandma and grandpa, then?"

"Yes, but we can wait before we meet anyone else. I think this is enough for now. It's kind of a lot to take in, isn't it?"

"Yeah," he said quietly. "My friend Carlton's parents are divorced, and he has to stay with his dad every weekend. Will I have to do that?"

"It isn't about making you do anything," she replied. "It's about..." She sucked in a breath. "I suppose we'll take it a step at a time."

"Are you going to make me hang out with him now?" he asked.

"Not if you aren't ready." She smoothed his hair. "I have a feeling you'll want to know him, though," she said.

Jack nodded again.

"And, sweetheart?" She put her hands on the sides of his face and smiled down into his eyes. "I love you. With all my heart."

"I love you, too, Mom." He wriggled out of her hands.

"Are you okay, sweetheart?" she asked tentatively.

"I'm going to read my comics," he said.

It wasn't much of an answer, but it would have to do. Jack needed to process things, and apparently he needed to do that away from her. It stabbed a little. "Sure," she said, hoping her smile didn't look as strained as she felt.

Jack ambled into the living room, and Sofia watched him go, her heart full. Had she done this right? Had she used the right words? Did he understand how much she loved him?

She closed her eyes and sighed, seeking her own comfort. She knew that God forgave her for her mistakes, and Jack was the perfect redemption of all the bad choices. He was a beautiful boy who showed her every day how God worked. Right now, she needed God, too. While Jack might be wary of having a father, she longed for her Father in Heaven to smooth this over and to bring them both some peace.

Her cell phone rang, and she looked down at the incoming number. It was Ben. She paused, glancing into the living room where Jack sat reading a book, then picked up the call.

"Hello?"

"Hi." Ben's voice was low. "I hope you don't mind me calling. Chief Taylor gave me your number."

"No, no, it's fine," she reassured him.

"How are you doing?" he asked.

"I've been better, to be honest," she replied with a sigh. "How about you?"

"I've had some time to think," he said. "I wanted to thank you for telling me about Jack. I know you didn't have to."

Actually, Jack looked so much like his father that it was only a matter of time before someone put it together, but she wasn't about to say that right now. Ben was trying to be agreeable, and that counted for something.

"It's okay," she said. "In fact, I talked to Jack about you tonight."

There was a pause. "Oh, yeah? How much did you tell him?"

"That you're his father," she said. She sank into a kitchen chair, suddenly feeling very tired.

"How did he take it?" Ben asked.

"Well…" She wished she knew for certain. "He's still digesting it, I think."

"Did he say if he wanted to see me?" There was hope in his voice, and she sighed.

"This is all really new to him. He's asked about you before, but this is the first time I've laid it all out for him, and I think he's in a bit of shock. He needs some time with this."

"Yeah, that's fair enough," Ben said, but he sounded a little deflated.

This was her fault, really. Her son had little interest in knowing his father because she'd never talked about him, never shown him any pictures. She'd told him that it would be just the two of them, and that they'd be just fine together. Then, after fending off all sorts of questions about the father he'd never met, she'd presented Ben as if he was supposed to be good news. Of course this would be a big adjustment for Jack. How could it be otherwise?

"I told my mom about Jack today," Ben said, and Sofia felt her heart constrict.

Mrs. Blake had never liked Sofia, and she'd made no secret about it. At first, Sofia had thought it was simple maternal protectiveness, thinking that no girl would ever be good enough for her son, but after a few months she'd realized that it went deeper than that. She'd always felt a little wounded about that when she and Ben had been dating. But she was no longer a teenager, and while Ben's mother's opinion of her didn't matter to her personally, it did matter to her when it came to her son. Shyla Blake was Jack's grandmother, and if his grandmother hated her, how exactly would this extended family work?

"Does she still hate me?" Sofia asked, attempting to keep the edge out of her voice.

"She's just protective," Ben said absently. "She'll be fine."

Sofia had tried to forget that with introducing her son to his father, she'd also be introducing him to the entire extended family. Sofia hadn't ever had to share him before. Even when it came to dating, she was cautious and didn't bring any men close enough for Jack to get attached. She'd lived near her mother in California, but it had felt natural to share her child with her own mother. Shyla was a different story. Shyla was a woman biased against her at every step.

"Your mom complicates this," she said. "Jack doesn't need the pressure right now."

"The pressure of meeting his grandmother?" Ben asked, and she noted the tension in his voice.

"Ben, let's just be straight here," she said with a sigh. "Your mother can't stand me, and Jack has just been told that you exist. This is going to be very difficult for him, and it will be harder still if he's introduced to a grandmother who hates his mom."

"And harder for you," he added.

"Yes," she said, her irritation rising. "It would definitely make it harder for me. And while we all want to make Jack the highest priority here, as his mother, I definitely factor in!"

"Hey, I didn't say you didn't. I was just pointing out that it would be harder for you, too."

She sucked in a breath and attempted to control her temper. She knew that Shyla was a part of the equation, too, and that scared her. No one happily handed their child over to bond with someone who actively disliked them.

"Full disclosure here," Ben said after a moment. "My mom is still mad because you left."

"I thought she'd be glad to be rid of me," Sofia said wryly.

"Yeah, me, too." Ben laughed softly. "She was always afraid you'd hurt me, and then when you left, she was proven right. I know you had every right to go—we weren't together then—but it was still hard for me. I know she can come off as really tough and thick-skinned, but deep down she just wants to protect me. You're a mom, too. I'm sure you understand that feeling."

She did, actually. Sofia would do anything to protect her son from being hurt, and the thought of some girl ripping his heart out in eight or ten years was agonizing. But this wasn't about Shyla's grown son; this was about Sofia's little boy. There was a big difference.

"I'm willing to have you get to know Jack," Sofia said, "but I don't want to include anyone else in that right now. And that includes your mom. Meeting his dad is big enough."

"I'm fine with that," he said.

"Are you sure?"

"I'll have to be." He was quiet for a moment. "So I have a question for you. How come your dad never filled me in about Jack?"

Sofia knew that when Ben had time to think this through, he'd resent her. It stood to reason that he'd resent the people who'd helped her keep her secret, but her father wasn't in a place to be handling anything extra on top of his cancer treatments.

"Because I asked him not to," she said firmly.

"So your whole family kept the secret?" There was a tinge of bitterness in his voice.

They had, and saying it out loud made it

sound worse somehow. They'd all agreed that keeping the secret would be best for Jack. Jack needed a certain caliber of person in his life, and his father hadn't made the cut. Her parents were just as happy to pretend that Ben had never existed. Once she'd moved to California with her mother, she'd never come back to see her father, either. It had been a tangled mess of strained relationships.

"Your dad and I actually saw each other pretty often," Ben said. "I mean, in a place this size it's hard to avoid people, but more than that, I think that I was the only one who really understood what your dad was going through."

"So you were friends?" she asked, surprised.

"No, not friends," he replied. "It was all pretty unspoken. But I helped him out when he needed it, and we—" He sighed. "It's a guy thing. Men don't have to talk these things through."

"Oh, I hadn't realized."

"So if he let eight years pass and never once told me that I was a father, you aren't the only one with a few grievances, Sofia. I know your dad didn't want you and me together, but once there is a child in the mix—" He didn't finish, but he didn't need to. She understood the point.

Their relationship—in any form—had never been supported by either of their families. She felt as if the room was getting closer, and all those old tensions from years ago were sweeping back in between them: his mother's resentment, her parents' disapproval and the fact that Ben was so much like her father that it hurt.

"Ben, I've been the center of Jack's world for his entire life," she said, her voice quivering with emotion. "This isn't about my dad, and it isn't about your mom. Not yet, at least."

"Agreed," he said. "This should be about you and me."

Just about the two of them…well, the three of them now. Wasn't that what they'd said over and over again when they were young, idealistic and dating? It should only be about the two of them, but they each came with families attached, and it turned out to be impossible. Sofia felt as though she was doing this all wrong, somehow. She was saying the wrong things and feeling the wrong things…

Because when she thought about what it was like when they were together, flouting their parents' expectations and passionately in love with each other, it made a part of her heart ache so deeply that she wanted to cry.

"We tried that once," she said past a lump in her throat. "It didn't work too well."

"Yeah." His voice was low and deep, so close with the phone at her ear, and she suddenly wished she could lean into his strong shoulder, smell that old scent of leather and cologne, and feel loved again.

"We can at least try to keep things between you and me," he said after a moment. "We're adults now. Maybe it will work better."

"It couldn't hurt," she admitted.

"I'm going to see you tomorrow, right?" he said.

"For the next two weeks," she said, pulling herself out of her reverie.

"Why don't I pick you up from your place in the morning? If Jack wanted, he could see me through a window or something."

She sighed. "Sure. But no pressure on Jack, Benji, you got it?"

"No pressure."

"Okay."

They were both silent for a moment, and then Ben said, "See you tomorrow, Sofia."

She hung up her phone and tapped it thoughtfully against her palm, then glanced up where the sound of her father's television filtered through the ceiling.

Lord, she prayed. *I have no idea how to do this well, or how to do this gracefully. Please, guide me.*

This wasn't only about Jack, it was about her, too, and the feelings that welled up inside of her when Ben's voice went low and soft like that, or when he flashed her one of his boyish grins. She was afraid of feeling more than she wanted to feel. That disarming smile, his easy laugh…

In some ways, it was like no time had passed at all, and her heart still went soft around Benji Blake. That was why she had to keep her wits about her.

While their son was forcing them into a closer proximity, she would be wise to remember her parents' epic fights: "If you hadn't been pregnant, we'd have gone our separate ways!" That's what her father had shouted at her mother while Sofia lay in her bed with headphones blasting music as loud as it would go.

She'd always vowed she would never give a man reason to say that to her, and that included Ben. He'd broken up with her for a reason all those years ago—they were too different after all, and breaking up was inevitable, he'd said—and Jack wasn't reason enough to change that.

Chapter Four

Sofia tossed her tablet, her phone and a granola bar into her oversize purse and ran her fingers through her hair one last time. It was silly that she was taking this extra look at her own reflection—something she rarely did—and she knew that it was because she'd be seeing Ben this morning. There was something about the man that he'd grown into that intrigued her in spite of her best interests.

This shouldn't matter, she mentally reminded herself. She knew exactly what her best interests were, and they didn't include getting her heart mangled all over again. She'd seen what that looked like in her mother, and she'd vowed she'd never repeat that pattern. She pressed her lips together to smooth her lipstick.

Her reflection in the hallway mirror presented plum lips and dark hair falling to her shoulders. She wore a tweed blazer with close-fitting jeans and a pair of brown boots. The spring weather outside was warming up but wasn't exactly reliable yet. Most of the snow was gone, but the puddles were iced over each morning. It was the kind of weather that was beautiful in the sunlight and cold in the shade. Dressing for it was annoying at best.

She dropped her lipstick into her bag and headed into the kitchen.

"How is your stomach feeling?" she asked her son.

"A bit better." Jack sat at the table, a bowl of untouched cereal getting soggy in front of him. His hair was still ruffled from bed. "How come you're all dressed up?"

"I'm dressed for work," she countered.

"No, you're fancier," he said, pointing at her face, and she felt the heat rise in her cheeks.

"I'm not fancier," she retorted, and picked up a banana and began to peel it, realizing belatedly that she'd only ruin her lipstick. She passed the banana to Jack instead.

"I'm staying home from school again today, right?"

"Yes, but tomorrow you've got to go back," she reminded him. "You can't miss too much school or you'll get behind."

Jack shrugged and fell silent. He took a bite of the banana and regarded her solemnly.

"I know this isn't easy," she said quietly. "You're being really brave about it all."

"Yeah, I guess." Overhead, the floorboards creaked as her father moved around. "What about Grandpa?"

Sofia glanced toward the ceiling and the sounds of movement. Her father was an incredibly complicated situation right now. "What about him?"

"Is he going to be okay?"

"I think he will. They caught it early enough, and the doctors are optimistic," she said.

"And they'd know, right?" Jack pressed.

"They'd know," she reassured him. "They're starting the treatment soon, and it will help him to get better."

She'd attended her father's last doctor's appointment where he'd been given instructions for his chemotherapy treatment. He was to avoid all alcohol and drink plenty of fluids. He'd also have to eat as healthfully as possible—something that Sofia was taking upon herself. His microwave dinners were out, and her home cooking was in. And if she was cooking for the family, he'd have to say farewell to gluten, too.

Her father's footsteps thumped heavily down the stairs, and after a moment, he appeared in the doorway. He had a ratty blue bathrobe cinched under his belly, his iron-gray hair flattened on one side.

"Why the uncomfortable silence?" her father asked with a wry smile.

"Jack was just asking about your treatment," Sofia said.

"Well, let's put it this way," he said, heading toward the fridge with a yawn. "You've got allergies, and I've got chemo. If it makes you feel any better, your stomach probably hurts as badly as mine is going to in a few days."

"It'll make you sick?" Jack asked.

"Yeah, but it'll make the cancer feel worse than the rest of me does." He pulled a carton of milk from the fridge, then turned to Sofia. "You realize Ben is out there, right?" He hooked a thumb toward the living room window.

There was a flutter in her stomach at those words—just nerves, she told herself—and Sofia strained to look through the small piece of window visible from the kitchen. She could see Ben standing in front of the cruiser, arms crossed over his chest. His muscles bulged in the long sleeves of his uniform—a definite change from his teenage years. With maturity had come a muscular physique. His expression was solemn—eerily like Jack's this morning—and she could only guess at what he was feeling. At least he was waiting outside, but it was obvious that he was hoping to see Jack, or he would have stayed in the car.

"Did you want to go say hi, Jack?" Sofia asked.

Jack shook his head. "Nope."

"We could go together," she suggested. There had been a time when having his mom at his side had made him feel braver.

Jack glared at her. "I said I didn't want to."

It looked as if Jack was starting to sort through his feelings surrounding all of this. Sofia met her father's gaze and read his disapproval there. Her father had never been a big fan of Ben Blake, and when they'd decided to keep Jack a secret from Ben, her own father had been more than supportive. She could see irony now, that she hadn't been able to see then—namely, that her father was adamantly opposed to the young man who was exactly like him. Her mother's warning, however, had been simple and to the point: bad boys might make exciting boyfriends, but they made lousy husbands. It had been her mother's words that hit the mark.

"Just as well, Jack," her father said. "We'll watch TV." He glanced at Sofia and put on his most innocent expression. "Something educational, right?"

"Dad, Ben is Jack's father," Sofia said, her voice low. "You, of all people, could be more encouraging about this."

"You made the right choice when Jack was born," his father replied quietly. "This here is stupid. Mark my words." He smiled grimly, then raised his voice to a normal level. "Have a good day at work, Sofia. We'll be fine."

Sofia sighed and crossed the room to kiss Jack's head. He smelled of Spider-Man shampoo, and she gave him an extra squeeze before giving her father a nod. "See you tonight."

When Sofia came out the side door, Ben was still leaning against the hood of his police cruiser. A brisk breeze rustled through the budding branches of the trees, and while Ben didn't show any signs of noticing the cold, Sofia picked up her pace and hunched her shoulders as she angled her steps out of the shade cast by the house and into the sparkling sunlight. Ben looked toward the window behind her, and Sofia shrugged apologetically.

"Jack still isn't feeling very well," she said by explanation. "So he didn't want to come out to say hello."

It was true, just not the complete truth, and she wasn't sure that it was fair to tell someone else everything that Jack was feeling. He might be a kid, but he still deserved his privacy. It seemed personal between herself and her son, somehow.

Ben pulled open the passenger-side door for her. "It's okay. Good morning, by the way."

In the window, the curtain moved, and Jack's pale, expressionless face appeared. She wasn't sure if Jack wanted to be seen or not, but Ben noticed her looking and turned, too. Ben waved, but Jack didn't respond. He stayed in the window, though, staring dismally out at them.

"Is he okay?" Ben asked when they were both settled in the car.

"He's still adjusting," she said.

"I can't blame him," Ben said. "I grew up without a dad, and I hated the guy for not having been there for me."

That wasn't a fair comparison, in Sofia's opinion, and she bit back her first response. Jack had always had his mother. He certainly hadn't suffered under her love and care. She'd been the loudest clapper at his school performances, and she tucked an "I love you" note in his lunch every day. Jack had always been a sweet and happy boy, nothing like his father had been as a kid, from what she could recall from their elementary school days, and she took the credit for that. Her son had always come first. She'd been a good mom.

"Jack isn't like that," she countered.

"Like what, like me?" he asked, tension edging his tone.

"He isn't an angry kid," she replied, refusing to be pulled into an argument about what he got from what side of his family tree.

"Yeah? Well, he looks pretty angry to me right about now. I know what it's like to grow up without a dad. Eight isn't too young to hold a solid grudge."

While Sofia could understand his new interest in Jack, especially knowing that Jack was his, that didn't make him an expert on her son. Their son. She was the one who had raised him, comforted him and listened to all his thoughts and feelings, and she was the one who knew him inside and out.

Ben looked over at her quizzically. "What would you think about me coming for supper tonight?"

"Are you inviting yourself over?" she asked.

"I'm not demanding you cook," he replied with a shrug. "I'll bring the pizza. Kids love pizza."

"He's allergic to pizza."

"Oh. Right. Is there any takeout he can have?"

"Not really."

Ben was silent for a moment, then said, "Well, never mind. Bad idea, I guess."

It wasn't actually the worst idea in the world, and Sofia went through her excuses in her mind. She couldn't avoid this forever, and every morning when Ben picked her up, she had a feeling that Jack would be silently watching his father from that window, feeling all sorts of mixed-up feelings. She had no doubt that he had a lot of things he wanted to say to his father, and because she was the one who had kept them apart all this time, she also needed to be the one to help them span the gulf. Whether she liked it or not.

"No, you should come for supper," she said.

"You sure?" He glanced over. "Do you think your dad will be okay with it?"

"No, he won't be okay with it, but, yes, I'm sure you should come." She smiled, attempting to look more certain than she felt. "For the record, I don't think Jack is angry with you. I think he's confused, and I think he's scared that having you around is going to change things between him and me."

"I'm not looking to change anything," he said.

Sofia felt a twinge at those words, but he was right. They weren't changing anything—not between herself and Ben, at least. Hopefully, Jack would have a dad he could look up to and a mom who was devoted to him, and he could grow up loved and secure. His mother and father didn't need to be anything more than co-parents.

"So where are we off to this morning?" she asked, changing the subject.

"I want to check up on Mavis Layton," he replied.

"Won't that be considered harassment?" she asked.

"Depends on how you do it," he replied with a small smile. "You don't give me enough credit for subtlety."

Sofia raised an eyebrow. "Perhaps I don't."

But Ben had never been the subtle type. He'd had the loudest motorcycle in town.

They were approaching a little subdivision called Raven Hill. It was built about twenty years ago, and she remembered thinking when she was young that the kids who came from the Raven Hill bus must be rich. It was funny how fifteen years could change a perspective. It looked like nothing more than a decent subdivision now, and the houses were slightly dated.

"So how are you going to do this subtly?" she asked as he turned past the Raven Hill sign.

"Mavis forgot something at the hospital, and I'm here to deliver it," he said with a grin. "What, did you think I was coming without a plan?"

Ben slowed as he approached the street that the Laytons lived on—Butternut Drive. It had such a homey, warm name, and the irony irritated him. But that was the way things were in a place like Haggerston. They were an idyllic community with cute streets, old homes with American flags flying out front, but behind all that charm were real people with real problems, and Haggerston wasn't immune. If there was one thing you could count on, it was not knowing what was actually happening behind closed doors without a warrant and bug.

The Layton house was an average-sized bungalow with a faux, 1800s-style street lamp perched next to their mailbox. Above their front door a wooden sign read: *This home runs on love, laughter and cups of strong coffee.* Patches of snow covered parts of a lawn that was coming back to life again after a long winter. Ben parked along the road and turned off the motor.

"So we're just going to knock on the door and say hello," he said. "Mike should be at work at this time of day, and Mavis is a stay-at-home wife, so this is the safest time to talk to her without her husband looming."

Sofia nodded. "Why are they still together?"

Ben sighed. "It might be against the law for a husband to beat his wife, but it isn't against the law to forgive him."

"And she keeps taking him back, obviously."

Why Mavis kept taking Mike back, Ben would never know. Mike was short, stocky and had beady little eyes that glittered like graphite when he was ticked off. Even his good moods came off as oily, in Ben's opinion. Mike was stronger than he looked, and he had a belligerent personality that only barely covered his gaping insecurities. His cocky attitude made big guys like Ben want to throw their weight around a little bit, based on instinct alone, and even more so when he found out what Mike did behind closed doors. Did Mavis feel sorry for

Mike? Did she love him still, after all he'd done to her? He wished he could make sense of that.

"All we can do is keep letting her know that she has options," Ben said. "The rest is up to her."

And a few well-timed traffic stops, he thought grimly. She wasn't quite on her own.

Ben opened his door and came around the car to meet Sofia on the other side. The cool wind lifted her hair away from her face, and he thought he caught her shiver.

"It's colder out here than it looks," Ben said. His first instinct was to put an arm around her shoulders and pull her against his warm side. What was it about Sofia that made their adolescent relationship feel so present? She hadn't been anything more than a memory for nine years, and all of a sudden, he had to stop himself from acting like her boyfriend just because a cold wind blew. He put a hand on her elbow to steer her across the water that rushed down the gutter, then pulled his hand away.

As they came up to the door, Ben glanced into the living room through the window. The curtains were open, revealing a neat room with an armchair, a big-screen TV and a lumpy-looking couch with a basket of knitting sitting beside it. It matched with the rest of the home, a veneer of a respectable marriage. Ben rang the doorbell.

Sofia shifted slightly beside him, and he could

feel the faint warmth of her arm barely an inch away from his. The soft, sweet scent of her mingled with the smell of earth and melting from the yard, and he sucked in a breath, pushing back the memories that all seemed a little too close to the surface lately.

It took a moment before he could hear any movement inside, but finally footsteps came to the door, and it swung open to reveal Mavis Layton. She was a slim woman in her forties, barely over five feet tall with a gentle smile and a cast on her left wrist. She put the cast behind her back when she saw him.

"Morning, Mavis," Ben said with a smile. "How are you doing?"

"Oh, pretty well, thanks," she said, an uncertain smile coming to her lips, her gaze flicking between Ben and Sofia. "Who is this?"

"This is Sofia McCray," he said. "She works with Mike, actually."

"Hi," Sofia said.

Mavis's friendly demeanor shut down. "What can I do for you?" She closed the door slightly, standing behind it.

"You lost an earring at the hospital," Ben said. "I was there on a call, and I overheard a nurse mention it was yours. I volunteered to return it."

"My earring?" The door opened again, and Ben pulled the dangling pearl from his front pocket.

"It looked antique," Ben said. "I thought you'd want it."

"It isn't antique. They're my favorites, though." Mavis took the earring from his fingers and stepped back, pulling the door all the way open. "Come on in, then. Thanks for bringing it back."

"Really pretty," Sofia said.

"Thank you." Mavis nodded toward the kitchen. "Would you like a cup of coffee?"

After wiping their feet, they followed her through the living room and back toward the kitchen. The rich aroma of coffee wafted around the house, and she lifted the coffeepot temptingly.

"Thanks," Ben said. "I'd love a cup."

"Me, too," Sofia said, sinking into a kitchen chair comfortably. She dropped her purse at her feet and gave a little shiver. "Sure is cold out there."

"That's why I stay in." Mavis poured Sofia's coffee first, and Ben realized that Sofia's presence here was actually going to be an asset. Mavis was warming up to her. "So you know my husband?"

"Not really," Sofia said. "I mean, I've seen him. I've only just started working for the paper. Ben and I know each other from way back, though."

"You from around here, then?" Mavis asked.

"Born and raised. Just came back after almost ten years."

"No place like home," Mavis agreed with a smile. She turned to Ben. "Oh, I almost forgot. Coffee?"

Ben smiled and accepted a mug. "How's your wrist?"

Color rose in Mavis's cheeks. "I know what you're thinking, but you're wrong."

"What?" Ben asked innocently. "I'm thinking that it probably hurts."

"Okay, you're right about that." She glanced toward Sofia uneasily. "Ben here thinks that my husband did this."

"Ouch." Sofia regarded her cast sympathetically. "Did he?"

"No, of course not!" Mavis shook her head. "I slipped on the ice out back. Another good reason to stay in, might I add."

Ben glanced out the back window. The backyard had a good amount of snow on the ground due to more shade, and there were a few icy patches still. He could probably give her the third degree and disprove her little fib, but that wasn't the reason why he was here.

"My husband has a bit of a temper problem," Mavis explained. "But he's working on it. He's a strong man who forgets how strong he is. That's all it is."

Sofia was silent. She took a sip of her coffee, her dark eyes filled with sympathy.

"You know how it is," Mavis prattled on. "The big louts need us." She laughed uncomfortably.

"Mavis, we all need you," Ben said with a grin. "You win the pie-baking competition every year at the fair, and I think you single-handedly organized the last bake sale to raise money for the Christmas hampers."

"Well..." Mavis blushed with pleasure. "I do try."

"Mavis," Ben said quietly. "You know you can call me anytime, right?"

She nodded, some of her confidence slipping. "Anyone can call the cops, can't they?"

"You know what I mean." Ben took a sip of coffee. She'd called him once before, asking for help when Mike was out of control, and he wanted to make sure that she knew she could do that again.

"Mike isn't as bad as you think," Mavis said, her voice trembling. "Ask anyone. He's a good man. He really is! He comes to church with me every week, and my sister's husband refuses to set foot in a church. So I know how good I have it—"

"It could be a lot better than this," Sofia said, gently touching the cast, and Mavis pulled her arm back as if burned through the plaster.

"Are you a married woman?" Mavis demanded, looking accusingly down at Sofia's bare left hand.

"No," Sofia said.

"Have you ever been married?" Mavis pressed.

"No," Sofia replied, and Ben thought he heard some sadness in that simple word.

"Then I don't think you'd understand," Mavis said, rising to her feet. "Marriage is complicated. It can be hard. It can be wonderful, too. But you don't just walk away from a marriage. You don't just walk away from a man!"

Sofia winced at that, and she glanced up at Ben apologetically. "I'm really sorry, Mavis," Sofia said. "I know you don't want to hear this, but you can have it much better than you do. And you deserve better."

"I think it's time you left," Mavis said tartly. "At least I have a man who comes home to me."

And who beats her up, Ben added mentally.

"I think what Sofia is trying to say is that if you ever need help, you know where to come," Ben said. "We're not going to judge, and we'll help you figure something out. That's a promise."

"*You've* been married," Mavis said, turning to Ben. "The 'I do's' are just the beginning, and it takes someone who has said those vows to really understand what I mean. No man is perfect, and no marriage is perfect, either. I'm sure you know about that."

Ben froze. He glanced toward Sofia, who stared at him in open shock. So, it appeared that her father hadn't filled her in on his life at all in the past nine years. He gave Sofia a tight smile.

"You're right, Mavis," he said quietly. "Marriage is complicated, but I never once raised a hand to my wife. Not once."

"I'm fine," Mavis said firmly, putting a protective hand over her cast. "I slipped on the ice. I'll testify to it in court, if I have to."

Ben had no doubt that she would. One more arrest for domestic violence and Mike would do some time behind bars. There was no way Mavis would press charges.

"Thanks for the coffee," Ben said, putting the mug on the counter next to the sink.

"Thank you for bringing the earring back," Mavis replied. She was the consummate hostess. "I do appreciate that."

Sofia stood, snagging her bag and settling it onto her shoulder. They headed toward the front door together. Just as Ben pulled the door open, Mavis put a hand out to stop them.

"Just so you know," Mavis said, a spark of defiance in her eyes. "If you try and make a news story out of me or my husband, my husband will be a very angry man. We're close friends with your boss, too, and he'd never let you slander us for the sake of an article."

Was Mavis warning them that she'd feel the brunt of her husband's wrath, or was she threatening Sofia with an irate coworker? Ben wasn't sure which, but he knew that Mavis was striking out with everything she had in her arsenal.

"Mavis, if you need me for anything," Ben said, ignoring the veiled threat, "and I mean that—anything—you call me. And don't worry. No one is going to do a news story about you. You have my word on that."

He glanced down at Sofia, waiting for her to echo her own reassurance, but she remained silent.

"Goodbye," Ben said, smiling at Mavis as reassuringly as possible. "Take care."

As they made their way back out to the car, he could feel Sofia's eyes pinned onto the back of him. The visit with Mavis had gone better than he'd expected. He knew that Mavis wouldn't be ready to throw herself into the arms of a women's shelter or to hire herself a divorce lawyer, but this was a step in the right direction. She had some fight in her still—albeit fight aimed in the wrong direction at the moment.

"So…that was a successful visit?" Sofia asked after they were settled. She reached for her seat belt.

"Definitely." He nodded, punching his own seat belt into its lock. "She liked you."

"Not at the end," Sofia retorted.

"Oh, what's a few threats tossed around?" Ben asked with a low laugh. "We expect her to protect her husband. This is the abusive dynamic."

"So, what exactly did we achieve there?" she asked.

"We chatted. We returned her earring. We let her know that there were other options and that if she felt out of her depth, she could call. That's a whole lot more than we could have done if her husband had been around. Sometimes it's less about laws and more about lives."

Sofia nodded slowly. "So this whole thing didn't happen, as far as my article is concerned?"

"Not if you want to keep her husband in the dark about our little visit," he replied tersely. "You print that up, even with fake names, and Mike will go straight home and take it out on Mavis. Guaranteed. Mike might be scum in my books, but he's no idiot."

"Understood."

Ben pulled away from the curb and followed the street around in a slow arc. Water rushed toward drains on either side of the street, and sunlight sparkled on the melting snow. A cat sauntered across a lawn, staunchly ignoring the passing cruiser.

"Ben, what did Mavis say about you being married?" Sofia broke the silence.

Ben inwardly winced. If her father hadn't filled her in about his life, it was only a matter of time before other people did. That was part of the challenge in living in a place this size. Privacy wasn't part of the deal.

"I was married," he said simply.

"But...when?" she pressed. "I had no idea."

"So your dad kept a few things from you, too?" he asked wryly.

Sofia sighed. "Apparently. I still want to know what happened."

Of course she did. And he couldn't entirely blame her. "I met Lisa my first year as a cop here in town. She was a new teacher in the elementary school. We got married about six months later."

"What happened?"

"She passed away a couple of years ago."

Sofia was silent for a moment. "How?"

"She died in childbirth—archaic as that sounds," he said, his throat tightening at the memories. "That isn't supposed to happen anymore. Our daughter was born too early and passed away a couple of days later."

"Oh, Ben..." Sofia whispered. "I had no idea."

"Yeah, well—" What was he supposed to say to that? Everyone else in town knew about his wife and daughter because they'd all been there for it. Half of them had attended the wedding. Sofia had vanished, not even bothering to keep contact with her friends from high school—he knew that because he'd asked them for the next twelve months if they'd heard from her.

"What did you name your little girl?" Sofia's soft voice pierced his reverie.

"Mandy. Amanda Jane, actually. I called her Mandy for short. It suited her."

"I can't imagine that kind of pain," Sofia said. "As a parent, losing your child—"

"It's bad," he said, cutting her off. How could you even describe that kind of gut-level agony? He was Mandy's daddy. He was supposed to protect her. He was supposed to be the wall between her and an unkind world, but there was no way to insert himself between his baby girl and the thing that was taking her away...

"What was your wife's name, again?" Sofia asked.

Lisa... He could still remember the look of hurt and betrayal when Lisa had confronted him with the letter from Sofia. She'd wanted him to say that it was nothing. She'd wanted to hear from him that he didn't feel anything for Sofia anymore, and he hadn't been able to say that— not convincingly, at least.

"Look, no offense, but I really don't want to talk about her with you," Ben said, his voice more terse than he had intended. Sofia visibly recoiled.

"Oh..." Sofia breathed the word out, then nodded quickly. "I'm sorry, I—" She let the word hang.

"It's personal," he said, in an attempt to explain. He didn't like to tell the story. He wasn't one of those widowers who welcomed the chance to talk about his late wife. Maybe he'd be more open with his memories if he'd done better by her, but he hadn't.

A call came through on his radio—shoplifting in the local mall.

"Let's take that one," Ben said, flipping on his lights and stepping on the gas. He picked up his radio as he hit the main road once more. "Ten-four. On my way."

He could talk about the hard things when it came to other people's lives—when he could offer a solution. He could talk it out with an abused spouse or a neglected teen, but when it came to his own issues and people in his own life, he clammed up. Especially when it came to Lisa—where no solution was even possible anymore. Times like this, the only choice he could see was to bury himself in his work.

Chapter Five

That evening, Ben stood at the front door to the McCray home with a shopping bag under his arm. He'd been in the natural foods section of the local grocery store for what seemed like an hour, trying to decide which packages of cookies were the best fit. Gluten-free. Nut-free. Dairy-free. Soy-free. Egg-free. Sulfite-free. There wasn't much left to the three different packages he eventually chose, but they were in the shape of cookies, cost four times the amount of regular cookies, and he hoped that his son could eat them. Which brought him to this doorstep, his heart hammering, wondering if a grocery bag of cookies was enough to break the ice with that solemn-faced boy who, against all the odds, belonged to him.

The doorbell bing-bonged from within, and a moment later the door opened to reveal Sofia. She was dressed in a soft skirt the color of creamy coffee and a pink top that flowed easily over her curves without revealing anything besides the barest hint of collarbone. Somehow, it still looked like the most feminine thing he'd ever seen. She'd always had that way about her—soft-lashed eyes revealing more than her neckline ever did, but still managing to leave him tongue-tied at the sight of her. He silently wished that his reaction to her had changed over the years. It would be easier if he could be indifferent. She tilted her head as an invitation for him to step inside, and stepped back.

"I come bearing cookies," Ben said, handing her the bag. "I wasn't sure which ones he could have, so I brought some options."

Sofia looked into the bag, then back up at him with a smile. "He can eat two out of three of these. That's not bad."

At least Jack could have something from him, and he cleared his throat, feeling suddenly uncomfortable. Having Sofia in his cruiser was one thing—that was his turf, and he called the shots. But here, in her father's home, he could feel the difference. He was the interloper here.

The living room looked different from when they were teenagers. The family photos were gone, except for a school picture of Jack with a toothless grin framed in something cheap and plastic. It sat on a side table. Steve had tried to purge Valentina from his home, but even without the pictures, she could be felt here, a memory that stuck with the persistence of a stain.

"So…" Ben brought his gaze back to Sofia. "How do we do this?"

"We keep busy," she said quietly. "At least that was my idea. Until we all feel less awkward."

"I can go with that," he murmured in reply, feeling a rush of relief that she seemed to have a handle on this, even if he didn't. She knew Jack, and she knew how to talk to him. He was starting from scratch with a kid who didn't much like him.

The house smelled of roasting chicken, and he caught sight of Jack standing in the kitchen doorway. The boy stared at Ben silently, reproach in his young eyes. He had those same soft lashes that his mother had, Ben noticed.

"Hey," Ben said, casting a smile in Jack's direction. "How are you?"

"I'm okay," Jack said sullenly.

Ben followed Sofia toward the kitchen, and Jack stepped back, watching them pass.

"I was hoping to put both of you to work," Sofia said a little too cheerfully, heading toward the stove where a pot bubbled on a back burner. "Jack, sweetie, get the salad fixings out of the fridge, and you and Ben can make the salad, okay?"

Sofia was trying, and Ben was grateful for that. As Jack headed toward the fridge, Sofia turned around and shot Ben a small smile. It was strange to be in this kitchen, watching Sofia at the stove, exchanging veiled looks with her as their son—their son!—pulled vegetables from the crisper. Sofia's hair hung long down her back, and made him want to grab a handful of it and let it slide through his fingers. He pulled his mind away from dangerous territory and headed to the sink to wash his hands instead.

"Where's Steve?" Ben asked as Jack returned with lettuce, a cucumber and three tomatoes.

"Dad will be here soon. He just went out for a walk," she replied. "He's used to having a lot more time to himself than he's been getting lately, so he escapes sometimes."

Ben smiled wryly. He had a feeling that Steve's escape had a bit to do with his arrival, as well.

"Grandpa doesn't like you," Jack said simply.

"Jack!" Sofia said, spinning around from the stove, her eyes snapping with warning.

"It's true," the boy retorted, undaunted.

"It isn't polite to say so," Sofia shot back.

"It's okay," Ben said with a laugh. "I already knew that."

Which was true. This wasn't news to him. When he and Sofia had been dating, her father hadn't been around much, but when they had crossed paths, the older man had made the most of his gun collection. Steve had never forbidden Ben to see his daughter, but he'd suggested, more than once, that Ben wasn't good enough for her. From this side of things, Steve McCray had probably been right about her being too good for him. Sofia had been smart, gorgeous and raised to succeed. He'd been angry, rebellious and self-destructive—but with a heart of gold, as his mother would have reminded him.

Ben accepted a knife and cutting board from Sofia, then set to work on the vegetables while Jack tore lettuce into a bowl.

"It's really nice to meet you, Jack," Ben said after a moment. "I know this is probably really weird for you."

"Yup." Jack continued tearing lettuce.

"You aren't too happy to have a dad?" he asked cautiously.

"I don't need a dad," came the reply.

That stung, but he understood the anger under those words. He'd spent his entire existence without a father. Suddenly, some guy was going to step in and be something to him?

"I get that. I didn't have a dad growing up, either. I hated him. A lot."

"Where was he?" Jack looked up, his brows furrowed. His dark fringed eyes locked onto Ben's face.

"I have no idea. He didn't want to know me," Ben said simply. "But I'm not like him. I really do want to know you."

Ben swiped the chopped tomato onto the salad and put down the knife.

"Oh." Jack's tone was noncommittal, and he reached for the knife and a cucumber. "How come he didn't want to know you?"

That was a question that Ben still thought about sometimes. How could a man know that he had a son and not even be remotely curious about him? Was the thought of responsibility so nightmarish that he'd rather stay in the shadows? Was his father still alive? Were they anything alike? Those were questions that never did stop, much like the resentment.

"He didn't want to be a dad," Ben said. "I guess. I don't know. I've never talked to him."

"Ever?" Jack asked.

"Ever." Jack seemed to be warming up to him over some mutual dislike of their fathers, it seemed. Ironically enough.

"You want to hear a joke?" Jack asked.

"Sure."

"So there was this boy, and he and his dad were eating lunch." Jack stopped cutting the cucumber for a moment. "And the boy asked his dad if bugs were good to eat."

"Bugs?" Ben asked.

"Bugs." Jack nodded. "The dad said that wasn't a nice thing to talk about at the table. So after they were done eating, the dad said, 'So what were you asking me about before?'" An impish smile came onto Jack's face. "And the boy said, 'Never mind. You already ate it. It was floating in your soup.'"

Ben barked out a laugh. "Funny."

Jack grinned, then he sucked in a breath, and the knife clattered to the table. "Ouch!" Blood squeezed between his fingers, and tears welled up in his eyes.

"You okay?" Ben moved to Jack's side of the table and eased the boy's fingers off the wound. It was a cut, but not deep enough for stitches. Still, it would hurt. "You have a cloth, Sofia?"

He was surprised at himself, how quickly he'd moved. That wasn't just police training, either.

Sofia came around to look, and when she saw the blood she blanched.

"Oh, sweetie—Jack, you aren't supposed to be using the knives." She looked ready to take over, but Ben didn't want her to. He could do this.

"I didn't realize that," Ben said. "He's okay, though. I'm going to show you how we cops take care of wounds, Jack."

"Yeah?" Jack asked, blinking back tears.

"Take a deep breath, McCray. You've got to be brave if you're a cop." Ben took the cloth Sofia passed him and pressed it around Jack's finger. "This is called applying pressure. Your mom will get us a bandage in a minute…" He kept talking as he worked, and Jack looked on in interest.

"Do you think I'll have a scar?" Jack asked.

"Probably," Ben said soberly. "A big, jagged one."

"No, I won't!" Jack laughed.

"You might. You can brag about it." They shared a grin, and when Sofia came back with the bandage, he wrapped it snugly around the cut. "Now, if you're a real cop, you have to fill out a whole bunch of paperwork for that wound, McCray. In triplicate."

"How come you call me McCray?"

"Because that's what we cops do. They call me Blake because that's my last name. And you're McCray."

"Oh." Jack looked pleased. "I'm not going to stop being a McCray, you know. Even though you've got a different name."

"I know," Ben said. "You can be my son and a McCray. That's okay by me."

Sofia came to inspect his bandaging job, and she ruffled Jack's hair affectionately.

"It's not too deep?" Sofia asked quietly. Ben found himself painfully aware of exactly how close she was to him...the warmth from her body emanating against his arm. She was near enough that he could have simply slid an arm around her waist—

He swallowed hard, pushing back the thought.

"No, it's not too bad," Ben replied, and he noticed that she relaxed a little at his reassurance. "Maybe I can finish up that chopping, though."

Sofia moved away from him again, and his shoulder felt cool where she'd warmed it by her presence. Ben sent up a silent prayer.

Lord, help me to keep this...

Professional? Distanced? Controlled? He wasn't even sure what he was asking for, but God did. This was one of those prayers where he had to trust his Maker to know his heart.

Outside, the scrape of boots echoed from the side step. Sofia glanced toward the door, recognizing her father's familiar sounds. These were the same scrapes and clumps that she recalled from her childhood, listening to her father coming in late at night when she was supposed to be sleeping. After a moment the door opened, and Steve stepped inside. He stamped his feet on the mat with exaggerated care, and when he lifted his head he looked directly at Ben and gave him a curt nod.

Sofia could feel the tension heighten like tightening threads, and she forced a smile to her face.

Don't ruin this, don't ruin this... If only her father could read her mind and take her warning. But all the warnings had already been given earlier.

"So you're here," Steve said. He took off his jacket and hung it on a peg.

"I am," Ben said.

"Dad, you're just in time." Sofia pulled the chicken from the oven. "I just need to mash the potatoes, and we're ready to eat."

Sofia shot a brilliant smile at her father, who ambled toward the sink to wash his hands, and she set the chicken on a pot holder on the table next to the salad. She stopped next to Ben again, her arm just brushing his, and gave him a sideways glance.

"Don't fight with him, okay?" Ben and her father had never exactly liked each other.

"Who, your dad?" Ben frowned.

"He tries to push people's buttons—" She stopped and headed back to the stove for the potatoes when her father turned off the water. She couldn't control this—and that was perhaps the hardest part.

In a few minutes, the four of them were seated around the table, Ben stationed across from Sofia, with Jack and her father on either side of her. She was sitting in the chair her mother always used to occupy.

Jack said the blessing, and the dishing up began.

"Pass the chicken, please." Her father didn't look at Ben, and Sofia passed the platter toward her father.

"So you used to go out with my mom?" Jack asked, and for a moment, all movement stopped, and Sofia heard two distinct ticks of the kitchen clock.

"I did," Ben said with a wry smile cast in Sofia's direction. The movement started up again, her father reaching for the mashed potatoes.

"Not that he was worthy of her," Steve said blandly. "Your mom was popular and smart as a whip. Your dad, on the other hand..."

Sofia closed her eyes for a moment and grimaced. It was starting... Her father hated that Ben was in the picture now, and he was going to fight this.

"Dad..." Sofia said warningly.

"If the kid is asking questions, tell him the truth!" Steve retorted. "Ben's got his life pulled together now, but back then he was a loser. He got into trouble, his grades were in the dumps, and you made a good choice in walking away. Don't feel guilty about that."

Maybe she couldn't control her father's antics, but she could certainly draw a few boundaries.

"No one's making me feel guilty," Sofia said, her voice only barely moderated. Her father managed to push her buttons pretty successfully, too, it seemed.

"Did you get into trouble?" Jack asked Ben, his voice low.

"Yeah, I did," Ben admitted with a nod. "I

grew up pretty poor, and I was angry a lot of the time. I got involved with some bad friends, and I made some bad choices."

"How come Mom liked you, then?" Jack asked.

"Because I wasn't all bad," Ben said, shooting Sofia a small smile. "I turned out okay, after all."

Her father grunted but didn't say anything. Jack was trying to make sense of this, and she couldn't help but wonder what her son thought of her right now. She didn't want him thinking he was the result of a meaningless encounter. Jack might have been unplanned, but he wasn't a mistake.

"Your father had a good heart," Sofia said. "And I loved him very much."

Ben glanced over as she said the words, his dark eyes locking on hers for a long moment. She felt the heat rise in her cheeks. It felt strange to be admitting to her feelings about him like this—in front of their son, in front of her father.

"And so you had me?" Jack asked, looking mildly confused.

"Uh, yeah," Ben said, swallowing. "It isn't supposed to work that way, though. We didn't do it God's way. If we'd done it God's way, we would have gotten married before you came along, but we didn't, and well..."

"So that's why you didn't get married, because I was born first?" Jack frowned. "I don't get it."

Sofia and Ben exchanged a frantic look. How did you tell a boy that he needed to wait until marriage for that kind of expression of love, when you had done the opposite, and he was the result of that mistake?

"No, it's more complicated than that," Sofia said, taking over. "But you did come along, and you were very loved and very wanted."

If only he could understand how much his mother loved him... There was silence around the table, the only sound scraping cutlery on the plates.

"I know you aren't asking my opinion," her father said, his voice low but carrying. "But this is too much for a kid his age."

Frankly, Sofia didn't care what her father's opinion was about this. He hadn't exactly been an exemplary father when he had his kick at the can, either.

"Steve is right," Ben said, exchanging a side-long look with the older man. "Look, Jack, things were complicated, but I now know I have a son, and I'm really happy about that. Okay?"

"Okay." Jack didn't look satisfied.

And that was that. The men had stopped the discussion. She sighed. Maybe it was for the best, but she wasn't used to sharing these child rearing decisions with anyone else, and it chafed a little. Perhaps she could have a private talk with Jack later on…explain a few things if he still needed answers. Ben might be Jack's father, but Sofia was the one who knew their son inside and out.

Everyone turned their attention to the food once more, and Sofia looked around the table at the men in her life. She was positively outnumbered, and if things were different, she might have looked at them with a wave of thankfulness. As it was, she was wary. They all wanted what was best for Jack, but she was pretty confident that none of them agreed on what that was.

The evening went more smoothly than Sofia had expected, and now that Jack was upstairs getting ready for bed, she felt a wave of relief that this first meeting was over. When she'd invited Ben so spontaneously, she'd been afraid that she'd regret it, but Ben had been great, and Jack had seemed to warm up to him, which was a good thing. Jack needed to at least know his father, and watching them together, she could see how utterly devastating it would be to her son if he met with rejection…like Ben had when he was young. Every child longed to be wanted.

Sofia stood facing Ben in the entryway. Golden light from a nearby lamp spilled over his features. He looked different out of uniform—more accessible.

"I think it went well," she said. "And thank you for what you said earlier."

"What did I say?"

"About him being a McCray and that being fine by you."

"Oh, that." He smiled awkwardly. "Well, he's yours, too. And you're the one who raised him. I mean—" He cleared his throat and looked away.

They had so much in their history—so much unsaid—that she didn't even know how to begin. She'd kept their son a secret and raised him alone. Her California friends thought of her as a single mother superhero, but standing here facing Ben, she felt like a fraud.

"I'm sorry." She felt the heat rise in her cheeks. "I'm really sorry that I kept him from you."

Ben moved toward the front door, but he paused with his hand on the knob. "What's done is done."

There was resentment layered in his tone. She couldn't expect a simple "sorry about that" to make up for eight years lost. There was no turning back the clock. Ben would never see Jack as a baby or as a toddler. He'd never hear that endearing little ducky voice asking for cookies, or see that toothless grin from the first grade. She'd wanted to keep all of that for herself, and she'd succeeded, only now she wasn't as convinced in her position.

"He's a lot like you," Sofia said, and Ben looked back at her, his dark eyes unreadable.

"Is he?" he asked.

"You don't see it? He looks just like you, Ben."

Ben opened the door, a finger of cold air touching her arms and bringing up the goose bumps. He wanted to leave, and she was trying to distract him into staying a few minutes longer. She wasn't being fair; she looked down at her painted toenails. He shut the door again, and she looked up uncertainly.

"Are we alone?" he asked quietly. She'd thought he wanted to escape, but perhaps she was wrong about that.

"We'd have more privacy on the porch," she admitted.

"Grab a sweater," he said, his tone low.

Sofia went to the closet and pulled out a thick, oatmeal-colored sweater. She eased her arms into it and wrapped it around her body, then met him at the door again. He opened the door wordlessly, and they stepped out into the night.

The door shut with a click, and the outdoor sounds of evening enveloped them—a distant rumble of a truck's motor, the swish of the wind moving through budding trees. The darkness seemed more comforting, too, somehow, as if not being able to clearly see his face shrouded some of their history, as well.

"To me, Jack looks just like you," Ben said.

"Does he?" She laughed softly. "I feel the opposite. I keep seeing you in him. He has this half smile he gives me when he's about to deliver the punch line of a joke, and it looks just like you. It's things like that—moments, really—when I realize that he's not all mine."

Ben was silent.

"I was wrong to keep him away for so long," she said. "I was scared... I told you that. I don't even know what to say."

"Look, it's in the past," he said. "At least Jack and I have met now."

"I'm sorry about my father tonight, too," she added. "I knew he'd be difficult."

"It's okay. I think he and I understand each other."

She wasn't sure what that meant. Her father had been downright hostile toward Ben tonight, and what two men could understand from that, she had no idea. Maybe it was just a mutual dislike.

"He hasn't had a lot to do with Jack, either," she tried to explain. "So it isn't like he took over any fathering role from you." She swallowed. She'd been furious with her father, too, when she'd left Haggerston.

"But your father must have at least met Jack a few times, right?"

Sofia turned away from Ben and walked

across the porch to lean against the railing. The front yard still looked the same after all these years, and her eyes traveled around her favorite spots to play when she was a little girl with a fistful of Barbies and her mother's good dinner napkins to use as beds.

"I was really angry with my dad," she said quietly. "He was awful. I know that's hard for anyone around here to see, but he made my mother downright miserable."

"What did he do, exactly?"

"He wasn't abusive like Mike," she clarified with a bitter laugh. "He'd never hit my mom or anything, but their fights... They were epic."

"Yeah, I've heard that divorces can be that way."

"I just couldn't forgive him. I blamed him for breaking up our family, and when my mom and I left for California—" She stopped. Explaining these things was difficult because family dynamics were subtle and conflicting. It was hard to make an outsider understand. "You see, my dad was only around for Sunday dinners. I didn't see much of him otherwise, and my mom was so lonely. Her entire family was in Italy, except for one sister in California, and she'd married my dad and moved here to the middle of Montana, and she was just so alone. Even my dad wouldn't stick around to keep her company."

Ben moved over to where she stood and

leaned down onto the railing next to her, his arm warming hers through the sweater.

"She always seemed like a bit of an island," he commented.

"I was her best friend." Sofia turned toward Ben and caught the shine of his dark eyes in the moonlight. "As much of a friend as a teenaged daughter can be."

"And you sided with her," he concluded. He reached out and put a hand on her arm, the warmth of it reaching her through the wool of the sweater.

"I did." She winced and glanced up at Ben. Would he judge her for this? She certainly judged herself. "I hadn't seen my father since we left town nine years ago."

"I guess it's more complicated than I realized," he said. He dropped his hand from her arm, and she found herself missing his touch.

"My dad isn't thrilled with me. He missed out on knowing his grandson, too, and coming out here is making up for a lot of lost time."

"What changed your mind about your dad?" he asked. A cool wind picked up, and she moved closer to Ben without thinking, looking for a bit of shelter. He reached out and moved her gently to the side where his body blocked the wind.

"Him getting sick." She tugged her sweater closer. "He called me to tell me himself, and he sounded scared. I guess I just realized that he was human after all, and maybe I was expecting too much from him. It's a hard day when you realize that your parents are mere mortals."

"Yeah, I get that."

"I just wanted you to understand that," she said. "Even though it doesn't make me look like much of a daughter."

"Thanks." He brushed a wisp of hair away from her face. "You're not as bad as you think."

"I'm glad you think so."

"Are you cold?" he asked.

"I'm okay." Truthfully, she was chilly, but she wasn't ready to go in yet. It felt good to be understood after all her years of worrying about Ben's reaction to what she'd done. Maybe she wasn't as terrible as she thought she was if Ben could see the good in her intentions.

"I remember standing on this porch." Ben shot her a teasing smile. "It feels funny to be back here, doesn't it?"

"I do remember that…" She laughed softly. Those kisses good-night late in the evening, whispered sweet nothings and giggling quietly so that her parents wouldn't hear them—somehow it didn't seem so distant standing here with him.

"I really missed you." His tone turned husky, and when she looked up into his eyes, she saw something there that she recognized from all those years ago—that glittering intensity that had always made her weak in the knees.

"Me, too..." There hadn't been a day that passed where she hadn't thought of Ben. He wasn't as easy to erase as she'd hoped.

"I'm going to have to be careful around you," he said, a smile turning up one corner of his lips.

"Why's that?" she asked with a low laugh.

He slid his hands up her forearms, his touch gentle and steady. He stepped closer, and she tipped her head back to look up at him. His lips hovered over hers, and she sucked in a breath. Was he about to kiss her?

"Because of this, right here." He didn't move any closer, and the few inches that separated them seemed like a gulf.

"What?" she whispered, but she thought she knew. It was all written in those dark, piercing eyes that were locked on hers, and her heart sped up.

"After nine years, you'd think something would have changed, but I still have to hold myself back from kissing you."

She swallowed hard, wishing she could just lean into him, feel his arms slide around her... But he dropped his hands, releasing her. It was just as well. They both knew better than to go down old paths.

Ben took a step back.

"So we still have a little chemistry…" she said weakly.

He cleared his throat. "I'd better go."

She knew that it was best that he leave. All the logic in her body told her to let him go—to keep that upper hand.

"Benji, wait—"

"Ben." His tone was gruff again, and he sighed and shook his head slowly. "Sofia, I'm not the same old Benji. I'm Ben now, and I'm a different guy. Those nine years made a big difference." He went down the three steps and turned back. "I'm sorry about all this. From now on it'll be professional reserve. I promise."

Then he strode out into the night, leaving her on the porch, holding her sweater around herself. What had just happened there? Sofia sucked in a breath of cold night air and turned toward the door.

Her mother had warned her years ago, and her words were just as true today: *Don't try to change a man. They don't change. One day you wake up and realize that all the potential you saw in him was just your imagination, and you are left with the man you married. No more. No less.*

A wise woman learned from her mother's mistakes.

Chapter Six

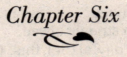

The next morning, Sofia chose a parking space as close to the oncology entrance of the Round-view Hospital as she could find. The low brick building sprawled out across spacious grounds. The emergency entrance was to one side, right next to oncology where the chemotherapy would be administered. Most of the paperwork had been taken care of already, and they were simply supposed to arrive.

Her father had been downright cheery when he'd chatted with the receptionist who called to remind him about his first chemotherapy appointment, and Sofia had wondered if he ever got tired of keeping up that jovial appearance. He wasn't cheery about cancer, but he seemed to take it upon himself to entertain the medical staff in his life.

"Here we are," she said. "You okay, Dad?"

"I'm fine." He unbuckled his seat belt and

heaved a sigh. His cheeriness was gone, and she thought she might take it as a compliment that he didn't keep it up for her benefit.

"I brought some magazines to read," she said. "I heard that it can take a while, and it helps to have some reading material to pass the time."

"Are you staying?" His gaze flickered in her direction, then straight ahead.

"I took the day off for this. Of course I'm staying."

"You don't have to." He looked toward her once more. "It won't be much fun."

"I know." Of course it wouldn't be fun. She shot him a smile. "It's like when I got my appendix out."

"Not really," he replied.

No, it was nothing like that. He was right. Her mother had been the one to sit by her hospital bed, reading her stories and bringing her Barbies to play with. She'd known that her father loved her. He'd stopped by once with a Big Mac that she wasn't allowed to eat that soon after the operation, and her parents had had a tense few minutes over by the door, their voices carrying easily to her bed. For some reason, they always thought if they turned away from her, she became conveniently deaf to their hissed arguments. She couldn't remember what that fight had been about. It was probably what most of them had been about—her father's priorities and whereabouts when his family needed him.

"I guess we'd better get this started," he said, pushing open the passenger-side door.

His words were heartier than his voice, and she felt a wave of sympathy. Her father had never been afraid of anything—not that he'd let on, at least—and she knew he was frightened now. The prostate cancer diagnosis had been a blow. Waiting for treatment to begin was even harder, in Sofia's opinion. Knowing that he had this sickness and having to wait for the cure... That was torture for anyone.

Sofia slammed her door shut behind her, and they walked together toward the oncology door. Her father moved more slowly than she recalled, but that might've been because of the thin sheen of ice on the asphalt, too. She put a hand out to his arm, and he shook her off.

"I'm fine," he repeated.

Out of the corner of her eye, she spotted a familiar couple coming down the sidewalk, away from the emergency entrance. Mike was talking to Mavis, his face too close to hers. Her expression was wooden, and Mike loomed over her like a vulture, whispering something angrily into the side of her head. She looked daunted and nervous, and anger rose up inside Sofia's chest. What kind of a man spoke to his wife like that?

"Good morning," Steve said loudly, before Sofia even had a chance to think of a plan.

Mike and Mavis both froze, halting in their steps, then caught themselves. They'd thought they were alone, apparently. Mavis shrank down a little smaller, and Mike's face melted into a wide smile.

"Good morning, Steve," he said heartily. "And Sofia—great to see you."

It was as if whatever had been transpiring between him and his wife had never happened, and Mike's full attention was now focused on Sofia and her father, his smile the wattage of a surgery lamp. He grasped Steve's hand in a firm shake and turned to Sofia.

"How are you settling in?" he asked, smiling condescendingly down into her face. It was too much familiarity, and she inwardly grimaced. She wasn't a child, but his demeanor suggested that he was much more grown up than she was—in his eyes, at least.

"I'm fine," Sofia said curtly, glancing toward Mavis. Mavis looked like a wilted plant, her eyes darting between her husband and Sofia, then down to her feet.

"How are things with that police officer?" he asked, lowering his voice confidentially. "It can't be easy for you. I know the police force wants to court the goodwill of this community, but officers like Blake make it hard."

"You don't get along?" Sofia asked innocently.

"He harasses my wife," Mike said, a dark look flickering over his face. "It upsets her."

Mavis shuffled her feet and pulled her woolen coat a little closer.

"Actually, we need to get going," Sofia said, glancing toward Mavis. Mavis looked stoically away.

"Oh, of course." Mike took his wife's hand firmly in his—palm to palm, not fingers intertwined. "We'll see you around."

Sofia watched them go, worry worming up in her middle. She'd never noticed how creepy Mike was before this, and she was mildly disappointed in herself for not noticing it sooner.

"I don't like that guy," her father said, turning toward the hospital doorway.

"Me, neither," she admitted. "I feel for his wife."

Sofia went inside, glancing around the oncology waiting room. Several nurses manned the desk, and farther inside, a semicircle of green plastic-covered lounge chairs sat. One was occupied by a woman wearing a red head scarf who had an IV in her arm. So this would be familiar territory for them for the next few weeks.

Her father headed toward the nursing station. He nodded to a nurse. "I'm here to be hooked up to the poison, ladies."

She smiled. "First-timer, right?"

"Afraid so, beautiful. Get used to this ugly mug, because you'll see more of it."

The nurses both laughed—giggled, almost. Steve had always had that effect on women. He was a flirt, although harmless enough, and likeable. Her mother had hated it. She'd wanted him to save his flirting for her, but that hadn't been realistic for Steve.

"You've got one last form to fill out, Mr. Mc-Cray," the nurse said. "Come this way, and we'll get you settled. You've stayed away from alcohol, right?"

"Sure have," Steve replied. "My daughter made sure of that."

They headed in toward the semicircle of chairs, and Sofia took the clipboard passed to her and scanned the blanks and boxes. The nurse settled her father into one of the green chairs and took his hand in hers. She flipped his arm over and ran a practiced hand up his forearm, patting here and poking there.

"Looking good," she said with a smile. "You have some nice veins for me. We're going to insert a PICC later on today, and that will make it so that we can hook you up to the IV without any trouble at all over the next few weeks. But we can do your first treatment by IV."

The other nurse wheeled a cart up to the side of the chair. It looked as if they were about to get started, and Sofia felt her stomach flip.

"Dad, I'll be back in a minute," she said, not waiting for his reply.

She moved away from her father's chair, turning her back on the procedure. She would be here for him, but she couldn't watch them puncture skin. That was too much to ask. She moved toward the outside door, looking through the glass, out at the icy parking lot.

Sofia could see Mike and Mavis standing by their pickup truck, next to a melting pile of snow from a winter's worth of plowing. Mike's anger seemed to be gone, and he bent over her in what appeared to be an attentive kiss. It struck Sofia as odd—that much public attentiveness in a marriage that well established. Perhaps the oddest part wasn't the attentiveness, but the enamored response from Mavis—as if she'd been starved for affection. From rage to passion. Mike never let Mavis get her balance, did he?

Sofia headed back toward her father, who now had an IV line hooked up. She stopped at his side and deposited several gossip magazines in his lap.

"You think I'm interested in celebrity gossip?" he asked.

"You will be by the time we're done here," she replied. "By the way, if you look at the celebrity cellulite on page sixty-seven, you'll feel better about your non-Hollywood figure."

"Me? Non-Hollywood?" He rolled his eyes at

her, and much to Sofia's veiled amusement, he obediently turned to page sixty-seven.

The next day, Ben parked in front of Sofia's father's home and settled in to wait. He'd spent the entirety of her day off kicking himself for his behavior on the porch, so that now he refused to even go knock on the door. He'd wait for her here, in his car, where he wouldn't make a fool of himself.

Lord, I've started over with You, he prayed. *Why is it so hard to leave the past in the past?*

The night of the dinner, Ben and Steve had spent a few minutes alone together in the living room. Steve had been smug about stopping the discussion about Jack's conception, and Ben had been annoyed with the older man's attitude.

"You're welcome, by the way," Steve had said.

"For what?" Ben had demanded. "For not telling me that Jack even existed?"

"It wasn't my secret to tell," Steve had replied simply. "And did you really want to tell that pretty wife of yours that you had a son out there?"

It had all come crashing down in that moment. While it might have been better for Lisa to know before they got married, what about afterward? What if Steve had sat him down for a chat after he'd said his "I do's" and dropped the bombshell that he and Sofia had made a baby together? What would that have done to Lisa then, when Ben would have been tied for life to Sofia, the woman whom Lisa couldn't seem to compete with?

Ben wasn't proud of who he was in high school. He'd not only been rebellious, but he'd also been taking his relationship with Sofia further than he had any right to take it without a wedding ring. Of course, he'd wanted to marry her in the end, but intentions didn't matter for much when it came to something like marriage. It was just as well that he never did ask her. It would have hurt a whole lot more having her hand back the tiny diamond ring he'd bought. Instead, he'd tucked the ring into a drawer and left it there—his last solid memory of the one who got away.

The side door opened and Sofia came out of the house. She wore a black leather jacket paired with charcoal pants. A bright pink blouse peeked through the front of the coat. Her dark hair fell in waves down her back, raven hair blending into black leather. She opened the door and slid into the car, a wave of fruity scent wafting with her.

"Hi," he said, waiting as she buckled the seat belt. "How are you?"

"Not too bad," she said, shooting him a quick smile. "My dad is pretty sick today, though. The chemo treatment was rougher than he thought."

"Should you be home with him?" Ben glanced past her, toward the house. The curtains were shut, the house taking on that dark, sad quality it had right after Valentina had left.

"No." She sighed. "He just wants to be left with a bottle of Gatorade and the TV. I told him if he called I'd come right back again."

Ben pulled away from the curb. "As long as you're sure."

"I'm sure." She eyed him for a moment, and he glanced in her direction. She hadn't mentioned their encounter on the porch, and he wondered if it had bothered her as much as it had him. He owed her an apology, and he knew it.

"Look, Sofia, I'm sorry about the other day—" he began.

"It's okay," she said.

"No, it isn't," he said. "I was out of line. What we were back then... I'm well aware that we aren't that anymore, and I wanted you to know that. Spending time with you, and coming to see Jack... That's not about trying to start anything up. I'm working toward cleaning up this town, and I'd like to get to know my son. It's pretty simple, really, and I have no intention of complicating it for either of us."

"I know," she said quietly. "It's just hard to forget what we used to be, I suppose."

"But not impossible," he replied. "It won't happen again."

He felt better having said it out loud. This wasn't easy working with Sofia and keeping things solidly professional, but just because it wasn't easy didn't mean it wasn't worthwhile. Maybe this way he could shed that lump of guilt he'd been carrying around in his chest.

"Jack really liked meeting you," she said.

"Yeah?" If he hadn't completely messed things up with his son, that would be a silver lining. "What did he say?"

"He seemed to connect with you not having a dad, either." She winced. "You know what I mean. Odd as it is, he feels connected to you because you understand a kid hating the man who wasn't around. I guess I was wrong about that."

She looked away as she said the last words, and he knew it was hard for her to admit. Sofia had always been a woman who knew her mind, and she was stubborn about keeping it.

"I guess you had to experience it," Ben said. "You always had your dad around, at least."

"He was around, but not much of a father," she said bitterly. "His friends came before we did. He was always helping a buddy out with something. He was the most popular man in Haggerston."

She was right there. Steve McCray had been everyone's best friend. He'd help you move, help you carry old furniture to the dump, fix your furnace… If anyone needed a favor, Steve Mc-

Cray was the one to ask, and all he asked in return was a few beers and a few laughs.

"So where are we off to?" Sofia asked after a moment.

"A basketball court," he said.

"Oh?" She looked over at him quizzically. "What for?"

"To play basketball." He looked her up and down, noting her high-heeled pumps. "Those shoes might not be the most practical."

"Oh, they're perfectly fine," she retorted. "I'm not playing. I'm observing."

Ben chuckled. He'd forgotten exactly how immoveable she was. He signaled a turn, his heart speeding up. This wasn't just any basketball court. It was the basketball court attached to the old community center where they'd had their senior prom. He'd seriously considered putting this off, but it was important, both for the kids there and for the article. People needed to understand that the real problem here wasn't ordering kids back to school, it was giving them a future to reach for.

"So, why exactly are we going to play basketball?" she asked.

"Because that's how to get to know the kids who hang out there when they're supposed to be in school."

He took another turn, heading across the tracks toward the old community center. It had been shut down a few years back when the new one had been built. The rusty old basketball court looked the same, and the truant students made use of both the shelter and the hoops.

Ben glanced toward Sofia uncertainly as he turned into the parking lot. She grew very still, and he could only guess that her memories were the same as his—their breakup right here in this parking lot. They hadn't even had a chance to go inside and dance together.

"So it's shut down now?" she said quietly.

"Yeah, in favor of the new one that was built," he said. He'd been glad when they retired the old place—it felt appropriate, somehow. "Look, maybe I should have warned you—"

"No, no." She smiled wanly. "It's been almost a decade. I'm sure we can put it behind us."

"Yeah." He wasn't certain what else to say, because she was being incredibly reasonable. That was exactly what they were supposed to do—put it behind them. He hadn't been able to do it yet—not all the way, at least.

A few kids leaned against the walls smoking cigarettes, and another boy was shooting hoops alone. They looked up sullenly at the sound of his engine. They were used to him now, so there was no scattering at the sight of a cruiser.

When he was their age, Sofia had made school bearable. He'd stayed in school for her, even if he hadn't passed all of his classes. His goal was to help these kids learn some lessons in a less painful way than he had.

Ben turned in at the old parking lot and eased around potholes until he came to the place he always parked, right within sight of the basketball court around the side of the small brick building. They both got out of the car, and Ben led the way toward the court.

He nodded to a boy he knew—Ethan—who lived in the same trailer park as his mother. He'd known this kid since he was in diapers, and it had taken some time to earn his trust after he started wearing the uniform, but they'd gotten there.

"Room for one more?" Ben called.

"I guess," Ethan called back. "You brought company?"

"She's a friend of mine," Ben said, glancing back at Sofia, who was just getting out of the car.

"She's hot," Ethan said, looking around Ben and toward Sofia approvingly. The other boys laughed, and one whistled, a few crude comments making it to his ears.

"Beautiful, yes," Ben said wryly. "Also smart. If you're going to impress a woman, you'd better broaden that vocabulary, Ethan."

Ethan colored, and the other boys laughed at his expense, seemingly oblivious to their own faux pas. Ethan passed the basketball to Ben, who caught it and took a shot. It hit the rim and bounced away. The game was on.

His uniform wasn't the most comfortable sports gear. His belt with his gun and other tools kept his arms from falling naturally to his side, but he was used to this and had adjusted his game to make room for his uniform. He'd been playing ball out here with the truant kids for the past couple of years.

Out of the corner of his eye, Ben noticed Sofia settle herself against the wall, her arms crossed over her chest as she looked on. Ethan sank a shot, and Ben sank one right after him.

"Does she play?" Ethan asked, looking admiringly toward Sofia. She had that effect on men of pretty much every age. Ben couldn't blame the kid for developing a little crush.

The ball bounced off the rim again and toward Sofia.

"No, she's more of an observer," Ben replied.

Sofia caught the ball and stepped forward. She was well outside the three point distance, and instead of tossing it back to him, she took aim. Ben gaped in surprise as she took her shot, the ball arching through a glare of sunlight and sinking through the hoop without even touching the rim.

"Wow!" Ethan breathed. "Did she just do that?"

The boys who were watching shouted in

shock, then erupted into laughs and jokes about a woman being better at ball than Ethan was.

Ben stared at Sofia with new respect. "Nice!" he said.

"I didn't say I couldn't play," she said with a small smile. "I said I didn't want to. There's a difference."

Ben grinned at her and shook his head. Apparently, a lot more than he thought had changed since prom. Sofia could now play ball. Maybe she'd be the better one to teach their son some moves on the court.

"Come, play!" Ethan called with a grin.

"I'm not wearing the shoes for it," she said with a shrug. "Just know that I could beat both of you. That's enough."

The boys whooped and laughed, and Sofia winked at Ben.

"Where'd you find her?" Ethan asked before passing Ben the ball again.

"At school," Ben said, taking aim. "A really good woman makes you keep up with her."

Ben released the ball, and it arched toward the hoop. It spun around the rim twice before dropping through the chain mesh. A phone rang behind him, and he glanced back to see Sofia pick up a call.

"School, huh?" Ethan looked toward Sofia thoughtfully.

"If you want a shot with a girl like her," Ben

said, "you'll need a thesaurus. A quality woman isn't impressed by being told she's hot. You'll have to come up with something better than that." He paused. "And for the record, you're too young for her."

Ethan grinned. "I know. But maybe she's got a cousin or something."

Sofia plugged one ear and cocked her head to the side, listening to whoever had called her. Her expression was grim, and her gaze flickered toward Ben.

"Everything okay?" Ben asked, tossing the ball back to Ethan and heading in her direction.

"Not really," she said, hanging up.

"Is it your dad?"

"It's Jack," she replied. "That was the school. He's gotten himself into trouble."

For a split second, Ben's stomach sank. For him, it had started with schoolyard fights. If there was one thing he hoped that Jack wouldn't have inherited from him, it was that touchy temper. Nothing good had ever come from it.

Chapter Seven

Sofia watched as the old community center slipped away outside the car window. Her stomach was knotted, and she sucked in a breath, trying to settle it back down.

She'd been surprised to see the community center looking so vacant and dismal. Her last memories of the place were at her senior prom, which admittedly had been a little dismal as well, but at least the Under the Sea theme had made the building look warmer. She could still remember sitting alone at her table, tears streaming down her cheeks while her friends attempted to console her in shifts. Sofia might be heartbroken, but no one wanted to miss out on all the glamour of prom.

"You guys always break up," her friend had told her. "He'll be back. He'll say he's sorry. He always does. Why don't you dance with someone else and make him jealous?"

She hadn't told her friends that she was pregnant, and she wasn't so sure that having Ben back was the right thing, even though losing him hurt more than anything had in her life to that point. She was having a baby, and Ben was defiantly committed to his motorbike. That was why she had been so eager to get some straight answers out of him. How *would* they do this? A baby changed everything. He'd dumped her before she even had a chance to tell him.

And here was that very baby, fighting in school. Just like his father had. She suppressed a sigh.

"I didn't know you could play basketball," Ben said, and she glanced toward him, pulling her thoughts back to the present.

"My cousin was playing for the women's basketball team in college. We went to college together. She taught me a few tricks," Sofia said. "Actually, I wasn't sure that one would go in."

"You impressed Ethan."

"Glad to be of service." She shot him a smile, which slipped away just as quickly. Her mind wasn't on the truant teens. She had her own child to worry about. The principal hadn't said much, just that Jack had been defiant all day with his teacher. It wasn't like him. He was smart and sometimes a little socially awkward, but not rebellious.

"He'll be okay," Ben said, as if reading her

mind. "Boys get themselves in trouble. It's normal."

"For you, maybe," she said bluntly. "Not for him."

"He's a boy."

"He's not like that!" A surge of annoyance rose up inside of her. "Why do you keep thinking that you know him better than I do, just because you're both male? I know my son!"

Ben was silent for a moment, and Sofia looked away, trying to tame the irritation rising inside of her. Jack hadn't been fighting before he met his father. Had she pushed things too quickly? Was he more upset than she thought? Had she missed something? It was her job to be on top of these things, and she'd been so busy with work—

"Fathers are necessary, you know," Ben said, his voice low.

His words slipped beneath her defenses, and her annoyance flared. Was he trying to say that she hadn't been enough for Jack, that her devotion and love had somehow fallen short?

"I've done well by him. I've loved him and supported him and struggled with the schools to get them to understand exactly how smart he is—"

"I didn't say you didn't do a good job as a mom," he interrupted. "I'm saying kids also need their dads. There are all sorts of studies that prove it."

Studies. She shot him an exasperated look. "I'm sorry that this took so long. I told you that I'm sorry."

"I'm not looking for an apology. I'm just pointing out that I might have some insight from time to time that might be useful. I'm not just some lump who donated DNA. As much as you might hate it, Jack is going to take after me, too."

She knew that. She was annoyed with Ben, yes, but she was more annoyed about the situation right now. She'd hated the superior sound of the principal's voice on the other end of the line, his tone suggesting that she'd fallen down in her parental duties if her son was behaving this way. And she'd likely have another few months of spontaneous meetings with teachers and facilitators who would think she was just another mother who was convinced that her child was better than everyone else's, trying to explain to them that Jack was much brighter than they were giving him credit for. The very thought was exhausting.

"Look, I know that you matter," she said. "I'm just—"

She didn't even know where to start with explaining how she felt about this. When your child went out into the world, you had to trust the world to be kind. But Jack tended to be misunderstood, and that didn't make the world a kind place for him at all.

"Why don't I come with you?" Ben suggested.

"Where, to talk to the principal?" she asked warily. This was not a good idea. Her first instinct was to give a decisive no, but she was trying to be diplomatic here.

"Yeah, why not?"

"Because it might upset Jack. He's probably embarrassed, and I doubt he'd want to be in trouble in front of a—" She bit back the word *stranger*. Ben wasn't exactly a stranger, but he was pretty close to it in Jack's life.

"If Jack is uncomfortable, I'll leave," Ben said. "But I've missed out on a lot, and I don't want to miss out on more."

"It might be better if you eased into this," she suggested. "Get to know him a bit more slowly. Jumping into the deep end of parenting—"

"You don't think I can handle it?" he broke in.

"I'm not concerned about what you can handle," she shot back. "I'm concerned with Jack."

"The community knows me a whole lot better than they know you, and I might actually be an asset in there."

Sofia paused. She hadn't considered that before, but he did have a point. Jack needed someone in his corner who could make the school listen, and who better than a police officer?

"Besides," Ben added, "I really want to, Sofia."

There was something in Ben's tone that gave her pause. He didn't look toward her again, just kept his eyes on the road straight ahead, but she could almost feel his hidden pleading. Ben wanted to be involved in his son's life, and while she still felt territorial when it came to her boy, having an involved father was good for Jack.

"Okay," she reluctantly agreed. "You can come with me."

"Thanks."

The familiar streets slowed in their flow past her window as Ben eased to a stop at an intersection. The light turned green, and Ben stepped on the gas.

"There are a few things you should know about Jack going into this," she said.

Ben glanced toward her and raised an eyebrow.

"He's really smart," she went on, "but the flip side to that coin is that he's not the most social kid. He makes a couple of good friends a year, but for some reason the teachers always point out that he can be a bit of a loner. Every teacher has suggested that he might be inching onto the autism spectrum, and I'd have to agree. He can really focus, and his brain can do things that other kids his age just can't. The hardest part is just getting teachers to understand that there is nothing wrong with him, whether he's on the spectrum or not. He's just…him. He doesn't suffer academically, and if he makes friends a little more slowly, that's okay. He doesn't have to be just like everyone else."

"He's more comfortable on the periphery," Ben said.

"Yes, exactly." She was glad that Ben seemed to understand, and he'd summed it up nicely.

"Nothing wrong with that." Ben shrugged. "He observes. He thinks things through. He likes time to himself."

"Yes…" She looked toward Ben, a mixture of relief and curiosity rising up inside of her. "You really do seem to get it."

"He's just like his dad." Ben shot her a small smile. "Except, without the motorbike. And maybe a little smarter than I ever was."

Just like his dad… Yes, that was the uncomfortable truth. Jack was an awful lot like his father, and maybe Ben could understand the boy better than she gave him credit for. Except, she didn't want her sweet boy to turn into a sullen mirror image of his dad.

"Don't take this the wrong way, Ben," she said seriously, "but I'm trying to spare him from that."

The school was approaching on the right, and Ben signaled the turn. Her heart sped up in sympathy for her son. She imagined him slumped on a chair outside the principal's office, feeling utterly alone. Had she made a mistake moving him out here to Haggerston?

She sucked in a breath, pushing that thought away. She'd know the situation soon enough.

Please, Jack, don't be too much like your father.

So Sofia didn't want Jack to turn out like he had. From where Ben stood—namely, on a sidewalk, walking toward the front doors of an elementary school in full uniform—he didn't think he'd turned out quite as shabbily as Sofia seemed to think. Frankly, Jack could do a whole lot worse than becoming a cop.

Underneath the insult, Ben knew what Sofia meant. She wanted Jack to skip Ben's difficult childhood and adolescence, and he agreed with her there. That was exactly what he was working toward in this town, cleaning things up so that kids could avoid his problems. He wanted to make the police force a place where people came when they needed help of any kind. He wanted kids to grow up safe and strong, not dealing with issues that were bigger than they were all by themselves. What made her think that he'd work for any less of a future for his own son?

Ben opened the door, and as Sofia slipped past, the soft fruity scent of her shampoo lingered near him. He wished he didn't notice things like that about her—the smell of her hair, the way her head came just up to his chin… The one who belonged in his thoughts was Lisa, and he found himself thinking about her less often lately—something that piqued his guilt.

The hallway was dim; the walls were made of cement blocks, painted a thick, creamy white. Overhead florescent lights hummed, and the voices of teachers and the chatter of children could be heard from behind closed doors. They were facing a windowed corkboard displaying some artwork from "Miss Paulson's Terrific Grade Twos," and Ben glanced over the dinosaur-themed pictures. One that stood out showed a T-Rex wearing a pink dress and a tiara. The name at the bottom was Amanda. He pulled his eyes away from it quickly. Reminders of his daughter like this one were coming up more often lately, and Ben sucked in a breath, attempting to steady his emotions.

"This way," Sofia said, and she led them left, toward the school office. He followed her, half a step behind.

This school brought back childhood memories of his own. He'd spent a fair amount of time in the office at school, kicking his feet against chairs while the secretary called his mom's various work numbers, trying to locate her. He'd never been helpful about that. It felt like his own personal revenge the longer it took for them to track her down.

This school office was behind a bank of windows. Two secretaries were behind the long desk, one on the phone and the other tapping away at her computer. Jack sat in a chair facing them, his misery evident by the long look on his face. He didn't raise his head as they came in, and Sofia crouched down in front of him, completely ignoring the principal, who came out of his office to greet them.

"You okay, sweetie?" she asked softly.

"I'm fine," Jack muttered.

"You got into some trouble?" she pressed.

"Yeah." Jack didn't seem keen to say more, but he did look quizzically toward Ben, and Ben couldn't help but wonder if he'd really be so much help in this meeting if Jack only clammed up around him. But he was here now.

"If you would come with me into the office," the principal said. "I'm Greg Heinrich. I'm sure we can get to the bottom of this."

Sofia rose to her feet and took Jack's hand. Ben felt a little extraneous, standing behind them. The principal waited until Ben had come into his office before shutting the door.

The office was smaller than Ben remembered with a row of file cabinets across the back of the room and two long windows letting in a slant of sunlight. There were some student pictures on the walls with "To Mr. Heinrich" written in child's script across the top. They looked fresh, so perhaps the principal swapped them out each year. Next to the children's artwork were some diplomas and a few awards.

"Officer Blake," Mr. Heinrich said, getting his name off his uniform. "Are you...?" He let the question hang.

"That's my dad," Jack said.

"Ah. Nice to meet you. Let's all just have a seat here, and we can sort this out."

Ben liked the sound of "my dad," and when he glanced toward Jack, he caught the boy's smile. Could it be that Jack was actually glad to have him here?

Ben knew most people in this town, but not having a school-aged child, he often missed out on a large swath of well-behaved citizens, including this principal. Mr. Heinrich was a short man, portly and white-haired. He sported a bushy white mustache, and he looked the way Santa Claus would with a shave. He also looked as though he was missing a cowboy hat. Maybe he wore one on his off days.

"We asked you here because your son was being disruptive in class and defiant with his teacher," Mr. Heinrich began. "We do have access to counseling here at the school—"

"My son does not need counseling," Sofia said pointedly.

"There are other solutions," the principal said, "but I'm sure you agree that this can't continue. Sometimes children need a little extra support. With this kind of behavior—"

Ben found himself mildly annoyed with the principal's obvious position. He leaned forward. "What were the circumstances?"

"Jack wasn't listening while another student presented a report, and he was sent from the classroom into the hallway."

"What else?" Sofia asked.

"While in the hallway, Jack was distracting other students, as well—" the principal began.

"No, I was asking Jack," Sofia said seriously. "I want him to tell me himself. What else, Jack?"

"I dunno." Jack slumped farther down into his chair.

"Give me a minute," Sofia said, turning Jack's chair to face her and leaning close so that her words remained private with her son.

"How well do you know Jack?" Ben asked the principal.

The other man folded his hands on the desk in front of him. "He's only been in our school for about two weeks now."

"Have you figured out how smart he is yet?" Ben asked.

"He's certainly a boy with gifts, but his teacher is concerned that he struggles socially," Mr. Heinrich said. Just as Sofia had told him he would. She'd been through this often enough that she could call it.

"How so?" Ben asked.

"Well, he seems slow to make friends during recess, but inside the classroom, he's been quite disruptive—which can be a sign that a child is overcompensating for social difficulties."

"He's new to the school. Of course he's not confident socially," Ben said.

"Hopefully, that's all this is, but we like to try and resolve issues before they become bigger."

Was Jack having some issues that needed extra help, or was he being picked on by his teacher because he was a little different? Kids didn't have to be carbon copies of each other. The principal was making this sound as if there was more to it.

Sofia straightened, and she put a hand on Jack's shoulder. "I want you to tell them what you told me," she said.

Both men stopped their conversation and turned toward Jack.

Jack licked his lips nervously. "I said a bad word to my teacher."

Ben stared at Jack in surprise. Here he'd been defending the kid's cause, and he'd been using bad language? He looked at Sofia, whose cheeks were flushed pink. She was embarrassed, he could tell.

"And why did you do it?" Mr. Heinrich asked quietly, fixing the boy with a direct look.

"I just…" Jack shrugged. "She doesn't like me. She always makes me do more math problems than the other kids, and she gives me different homework."

Ben couldn't help the smile that came to his face. So the teacher had figured out just how smart he was! Jack wasn't used to that, apparently.

"Your teacher is trying to give you a challenge in your schoolwork," Mr. Heinrich said. "You're a bright boy. You're ahead of your class in almost every subject."

"I don't need a challenge, I need friends." Jack's voice was so low that Ben almost didn't hear him, and he felt a wave of pity for the kid. He was definitely smart, but he was tired of being different. Ben had always felt different, too, but for different reasons. He'd been poor.

"Your teacher was giving you more advanced work?" Sofia asked. "Jack, this is wonderful! Finally, a teacher who sees what you can do!"

"Maybe I don't want to do more," Jack retorted. "It's not fair."

"Who do you play with?" Ben asked.

"I don't know."

"Anyone?" Sofia asked, and he saw tears rise in her eyes.

"I don't remember." Jack wasn't going to answer this one, and Ben could guess why. When he was an eight-year-old, he'd struggled with making friends, too, and he'd hidden it behind a facade of anger and indifference.

"Maybe we could ease back on the academic challenges," the principal said. "Now, as for the language—"

"He did not learn that at home," Sofia said briskly.

"When students show verbal aggression, we have a special work group where we teach kids how to communicate more effectively. I think Jack would benefit from it."

Sofia turned to Ben and raised her eyebrows. "What do you think?"

Ben was surprised to have her consult him, but it felt good, too. Maybe she was beginning to trust him just a little bit more when it came to their son. Her trust would be hard-won, but he was determined to gain it. This looked like a step in the right direction.

"I'll give you a moment," the principal said, rising to his feet. He left the office and closed the door behind him.

Sofia shook her head. "I don't want them to start treating him like a problem kid," she said. "He's not one! And I won't have him streamed in that direction. He's an excellent reader, and he gets A's on all his written work. He communicates just fine."

"This isn't really about problems with communication," Ben said. "This is about consequences for his actions. He used bad language. If the teacher thought less of him, she wouldn't have made such a big deal out of it. Trust me. No one even blinked when I swore in school, and I had the mouth of a pint-sized sailor. They see promise in Jack, and they won't let him slide off into delinquent behavior. I don't think you need to worry that they'll start seeing him as a bad kid."

"I'm sorry, Mom," Jack muttered.

"Swearing is bad, I agree," Ben said. "And he's learned something." He fixed Jack with a thoughtful look. "Jack, what if I showed you a few techniques we cops use to defuse situations?"

Sofia gave him a funny look. "He's not going to be breaking up fights. He just needs to watch his mouth."

But Ben wasn't deterred. Jack didn't just need to learn how to behave, he needed to learn how to deal with it all. That was part of growing up, and this was something he could offer. Finally.

"I'm not going to teach him how to cuff people." Ben grinned at Jack. "Sorry about that, Jack. All he needs is a bit of confidence, and I can show him some tricks."

Sofia brightened marginally. "That actually sounds good."

"Okay," Jack said with more enthusiasm than his mother showed. "I'd like that. Could you show me how to use the cuffs, too, though?"

"No to the cuffs, and you're still going to have to do your time in that nonaggressive communication group." Ben made a face. "Sounds boring, but you earned it."

"Yeah, I can do that." Jack grinned. "Thanks."

They were silent for a moment, and he looked over at Sofia. Her dark lashes veiled her eyes, and she looked down at the carpet frowning. Sofia raised her head and met Ben's gaze.

"Okay," she said after a moment. "I'll sign the form."

It made sense to Ben. Facing the consequences of his behavior was good for a boy. It wasn't terrible for his social standing with the other boys in class, either. Jack would be all right.

"You had a good instinct there," she said after a moment.

"I'm more useful than I look," Ben said with a wry smile.

She rolled her eyes and turned toward the door, ignoring his last comment. He grinned at her back.

"Come on, Jack," she said. "You need to get back to class."

This was about as close as Sofia had come to allowing him to be a support to them both, and he felt strangely optimistic about it. He might not have been around for the past eight years of Jack's life, but it turned out that a dad did know a thing or two, after all.

I would have been good at this, he thought to himself. If he'd still had Lisa and little Mandy, he would have been a good dad. It was his role of husband that had fallen short. Maybe it was better to keep things like this—be a father to his son and not inflict himself as a husband on anyone else. He'd keep to his strengths.

Chapter Eight

That evening, Sofia pushed the grocery cart down the aisle of Bounty Foods. It had been an emotionally tumultuous day, and she was ready to pick up some groceries and go home. She was even going to skip the treadmill tonight and go straight for the tube of frozen cookie dough in the back of the freezer—the kind that Jack was allergic to, and that she could only dig out after he was in bed. She needed some comfort food and some time to herself—the combination that always helped her through hard times in the past, but her duties in taking care of her family weren't done for the day. While laundry could wait, the groceries couldn't. They were down to crumbs.

Her father seemed to have stopped eating completely, his stomach horribly upset from his chemo treatment. The spot on his arm where the IV went in was bruised, and he would sip meal replacement shakes and bottles of juice, but he complained that everything tasted terrible now and couldn't even choke down water.

She wanted to find something her father could eat... Pudding, maybe? Canned fruit? She'd bring home some options and hope that something worked.

Jack seemed unfazed by the day's events, and he was ambling along behind her, looking for his favorites to add to the cart. His rubber boots thunked along the floor, out of rhythm with the canned country music playing in the background. The grocery store wasn't a big one, but it was well stocked and was conveniently located in downtown Haggerston. There were bigger stores in the next town over, but Sofia didn't have the energy right now to plan for extended shopping trips. What with her job, Jack and helping her father with his medical appointments, her energy was used up.

"We should get cookies today," Jack said.

"We just had cookies when Ben came over."

"We should get more."

"We'll see how much money we have left," she replied absently. In her opinion, her son wasn't too young to know about budgets and the fact that money ran out. Being a single mother, she had to be smart with her dollars, and he'd have to learn the same skills.

"What about the coconut milk ice cream?" he asked.

"Same answer, kiddo." She glanced back and gave him a smile. "You'll survive on healthy food. It won't kill you. I promise."

Jack heaved a sigh. Such a cruel, cruel mother. She smirked to herself.

Sofia rounded a corner, heading toward the next aisle. She paused to grab a couple cartons of almond milk from the refrigerated dairy case. She read the ingredients quickly, just making sure nothing had changed. That was one of the challenges with allergies—they were at the mercy of the factories and those cocktails of ingredients that could change without warning.

This isn't easy, Lord, she prayed. *I'm so tired...*

Sofia was glad that Ben had been with her at the school that day. She'd been certain that she wanted to handle the meeting alone, but he'd turned out to be useful—both in offering to teach Jack some confidence-building techniques, and in calming her down. She hated to admit that his presence had helped. Having so much on her shoulders meant that something like her son getting into trouble felt bigger and heavier than it needed to, and she would hate to pass that burden on to Jack without meaning to.

Was it a sign of weakness that she was starting to wish she had someone to help share those burdens?

Sofia grabbed a jug of regular milk for herself and her father and dropped it into the cart, then headed in the direction of the next aisle where the cereal was located. A voice behind her drew her attention.

"Are you Jack?"

Her protective instinct tingled, and she turned around, stopping short. A petite woman with teased brown hair stood staring at Jack. She wore a pair of leopard-print leggings and held a loaf of bread in one hand, but her attention was riveted to Jack's face. It was Shyla Blake, Ben's mother.

"Shyla," Sofia said, attempting to cover the surprise in her tone.

"This *is* Jack, right?" Shyla's gaze flickered from Sofia, back to the boy. She stepped closer, her red lipsticked lips parting as if she wanted to say more, and her eyes moving over his face.

This was not the timing that Sofia had wanted. She'd been nudged into revealing Jack's father earlier than she'd planned because of circumstances, but she'd been incredibly clear about where she stood on Ben's mother. After the day she'd just had, irritation simmered very close to the surface.

"Shyla, this isn't a great time," Sofia said, warning in her tone.

"No?" Shyla shot back. "When would be? Because it's been eight years."

"Who is this, Mom?" Jack asked uneasily.

"You, of all people, should understand this!" Sofia retorted, ignoring Jack's question. "We have a lot going on right now, and later would be better."

She said the last words slowly and clearly. Shyla was a single mother, too, so she should understand a mother's protectiveness, even if she didn't agree with it. A mother knew better than to try and lever her way between another mom and her child.

"You never told me." Shyla's voice shook, and she turned her attention to Sofia. "Did you know I lost a grandchild?"

"I only found out recently. I'm very sorry for your loss."

The thought of the baby who had died was terrible. Sofia could understand Shyla's grief, but that couldn't be dumped onto the shoulders of a little boy, either.

"So you'd understand then, how much this would mean to me," Shyla said.

"Mom, who is this?" Jack repeated, and Sofia looked down at him, wondering how much to say. She'd been backed into a corner here. Jack had obviously just met Shyla, so there was no pretending it hadn't happened. Hadn't Ben told his mother about her request for some time? Or did Shyla simply not care?

"I'm your grandma. Maybe granny. I haven't decided yet." Shyla sucked in a deep breath. "I'm your father's mother. I've been very eager to meet you, Jack."

"My grandma?" Jack looked over at Sofia.

"Yes. This is Ben's mom. I was hoping we could have a little more time with Ben before we expanded to extended family, but it looks like we ran into each other."

Shyla shrugged and smiled sweetly. "It's a small town. These things happen."

Sofia highly doubted that this meeting was completely random. Shyla smiled warmly at Jack and held out her hand to shake his. Jack took it, and instead of shaking, Shyla simply held his hand in hers tenderly.

"You look a lot like your father did at your age," she said. "He always was a good-looking boy."

"My mom said I looked like him a bit," Jack said.

"More than a bit." Shyla shot Sofia an indecipherable look, then turned her attention back to Jack. "I have all sorts of pictures of your dad when he was young, if you'd like to see them. You seem to take after our side of the family."

"Yeah, I'd like to see pictures." Jack looked up at his mother questioningly.

"We'll see," Sofia said noncommittally. This would not be happening soon, if she could help it. They were dealing with enough right now.

"Did your mother tell you about us?" Shyla pressed, and Jack shook his head. "If we'd known about you, I could have been sending you birthday presents and Christmas presents all this time. I promise you, Jack, I didn't know about you. I don't want you think that I didn't care."

"Thanks, Shyla, I think we're clear on that," Sofia said quickly. They were standing in the middle of a grocery store, and a man pushed his cart past them, glancing at them in curiosity. This was the sort of meeting that should be happening with some privacy and with some warning. There were things she'd wanted to explain to Jack first, but she no longer had that chance.

"Maybe Jack could come over to see me one of these days," Shyla suggested.

Shyla wanted Jack, not Sofia—that much was clear. Perhaps Sofia was being a little unfair, but after the way Shyla had treated her back in high school, she wasn't sure what to expect.

"We'll have to see," Sofia repeated, and silently, she sent up a prayer for wisdom.

"Could my mom come, too?" Jack asked, and Sofia couldn't help the smile that came to her lips. Sofia ruffled her son's hair lovingly. Good, sweet Jack. It wasn't that he was trying to protect his mother or look out for her. He wouldn't even pick up on the complicated tensions between herself and Ben's mother, but Jack simply needed her still, and that was quite enough to fill her heart.

Shyla paused for a beat. "I thought you might want to come with your dad."

Sofia wasn't sure what expression was on her face, but when Shyla looked at her, she froze for a moment, and then continued, "I have something for you."

Shyla reached into her purse and pulled out her wallet. She took out several bills and pressed them into Jack's hand. When Sofia looked closer, she saw that it was two fifties, a twenty and a one.

"Shyla, that really isn't necessary," Sofia said, shaking her head. First of all, it was too much for an eight-year-old, and secondly, a mother should be consulted before her child was given cash.

"Of course, it is," Shyla retorted. "Don't ruin his fun. That's to make up for all those missed birthdays. I won't be missing them from now on."

"Thank you!" Jack said jubilantly. He beamed at his grandmother and then looked down at the money in his hands again. "Can we go buy some toys, Mom?"

Sofia shut her eyes for a moment, looking for some calm. It was beginning. Shyla had pushed herself into the middle, and now she would start buying Jack's affection with cash and gifts. She understood that grandparents enjoyed spoiling their grandkids, but she had a sinking suspicion that this wasn't going to be an easy road. Shyla felt she'd been wronged by not knowing about Jack, and that wouldn't improve her opinion of Sofia one bit.

"When is his birthday?" Shyla asked.

"It's February eleven," Jack said. "I'm eight now."

"I'll remember that." Shyla tapped the side of her head and smiled.

"We need to get going," Sofia said, and Shyla, for the first time, seemed to take the hint.

"Of course," she said, then reached out and put a hand on Jack's cheek. "I'll see you soon, Jack."

Sofia didn't miss the fact that Shyla didn't even bother saying goodbye to her. And as they moved down the cereal aisle, Sofia attempted to calm her nerves.

"That's my grandma?" Jack asked, his voice carrying.

"Yes." Sofia stopped and bent down. "Jack, please, talk quietly. We don't want everyone hearing this."

"Okay." Jack lowered his volume. "Are we going to visit her?"

"I imagine we will, sweetie," she said quietly,

"but we need to do one thing at a time. Right now, you're taking some time to get to know your dad."

"Oh." Jack didn't look convinced. "You don't like her, do you?"

Sofia felt the tears rise up inside of her, and she fought to keep them down. This was what her son took away from this meeting, that she didn't like his grandmother? Was she supposed to tell him how much Shyla disliked her, or did she just let him figure that out in due time?

"It isn't that," Sofia said quietly. "I've just had a really hard day today, and I want to get home and make supper."

Sofia scanned her grocery list. There were a few items left on it, but they'd just have to wait. She crumpled the paper and dropped it into her pocket.

"Let's go pay," she said.

All she wanted was to get home where it was warm and quiet and out of public sight. Later on tonight after Jack was in bed, she'd wrap herself up with a blanket on the couch and spend some time with her Bible. Some comfort needed to come straight from the Source. Cookie dough wasn't going to cut it.

Ben sank into his chair in front of his desk at the police station and pulled out a stack of unfinished forms. If there was one thing he hated in this job, it was the constant filing. There were forms for pretty much everything, and they needed to be filled out in triplicate.

The station was relatively empty at this time of day. The day shift had gone home, and the night shift was already out on patrol. Officer Tate was sticking around to man the station, and Ben was making use of the quiet.

Truthfully, he was doing more than filing; he was processing his own thoughts. He wasn't ready to go home yet. Professional surroundings were like armor; they made him feel stronger than he did sitting by himself in his own home.

Home had taken on a new meaning since he lost his family. Before he met Lisa, home was a place to kick back and relax. He hosted barbeques, had the guys over to watch a game or just hung out by himself. When he got married, though, home became something much deeper and warmer. Home was where his wife was. His home became filled with all the little things that mark a woman's presence—scented soaps, matching towels, good china. He had wedding pictures on the walls, and he was assigned a side to the bed. The guys came over a lot less often, and he didn't mind as much as he thought he would. Home was no longer his; it was his and Lisa's.

When he lost Lisa and Mandy, home suddenly felt like a cave—empty and echoing. He hated being there because it reminded him of everything he was missing.

"Hey, Blake."

Ben looked up to see the chief coming toward him. Chief Taylor pulled up a chair opposite Ben's desk and sat down, giving Ben a smile.

"How's it going, Chief?" Ben said. "As you can see, I'm catching up."

Ben was consistently on the verge of being behind in his paperwork, and he got reminded every so often to get on top of it. He was happier in a squad car, out there with the community, and paperwork always felt as if it slowed him down.

"I have enough of my own right now." Chief Taylor paused, then cleared his throat. "So how is it going with the journalist?"

"Not too badly."

"I heard a rumor, actually."

"Oh, yeah?" Ben eyed his boss curiously. He wasn't about to offer any personal information right now, but he was curious to see what the scuttlebutt around town might be.

"You told me that you and Miss McCray had dated back in the day, but I heard recently that you two actually have a child together. Is that true?"

Ben exhaled a pent-up breath.

"How did you hear that?"

"Your aunt, Esther Blake, actually." The chief

looked mildly embarrassed. So his mother had been telling her closest confidants, it appeared. Word was officially out.

"Yes, it is true," he said. "I only found out recently, and I didn't know that word was travelling yet. It was news to me, too, for the record."

"I apologize for not taking you more seriously when you stated your concerns about working with her," the chief said seriously. "I thought it was just small-town drama. I hadn't realized it was this complicated for you."

"Neither had I," Ben said. "When I voiced my concerns, I didn't know about my son."

"If you'd rather have her assigned to someone else, we can do that," Chief Taylor said. "I wouldn't want to compromise this project, or your professionalism, for that matter."

Ben was silent for a moment, his mind working in circles. If the chief had given him this option a week ago, he would have jumped at it, but things were different now. Not only did he want to get to know his son better, but this time with Sofia was turning out to be the bright part of his week. Besides, he'd only been able to attend that meeting at his son's school because he'd been working with Sofia at the time. If they parted company now, he had a feeling he'd miss out on a whole lot more that Sofia would never tell him about.

"I'm actually doing okay, Chief," Ben said

after a moment. "We're both adults, and we're conducting ourselves as professionals."

For the most part, he thought wryly, remembering the evening on the porch when she'd been so warm and near, and he'd been so tempted to close that distance between them. But that wouldn't be happening again.

"You don't think your personal history will… color her journalism?"

"Not Sofia." Ben smiled ruefully. "Besides, I'm behaving myself."

"Good to hear," his boss said, pushing himself to his feet. "If you change your mind and want me to assign her to someone else, let me know."

"Sure thing. Thanks, Chief."

The station's front door opened, and Mrs. Taylor poked her head inside. She was a young woman, no more than thirty, with chestnut hair pulled back in a ponytail. A redheaded toddler squeezed ahead of her mother and ran through the station. "Daddy!" she squealed. She collided with the chief's legs and held her arms up, and the chief's face melted into a grin. He scooped her up and planted some kisses on her cheek, walking toward his waiting wife at the door.

Ben bent back down over his work. Chief Taylor had it good, but Ben knew better than to waste his energy envying another man's blessings. It would get easier with time. Wasn't that what he always told the people who were hitting bottom, that time would make it better? He'd just have to wait it out.

Ben clicked over to his email on the computer and selected a few messages to go straight to the trash. He was tired already, and he rubbed his hands over his eyes. His phone rang, and he glanced at the number before picking it up.

"Hi, Mom," he said, stifling a yawn.

"I had an interesting day," his mother said. "Do you want to hear what happened?"

"Sure." Ben turned back to his emails and opened a bulletin the chief had sent out earlier that day that he hadn't had a chance to read yet. His eyes scanned the pertinent details, then he clicked on Delete.

"I met my grandson." Her voice was almost crowing, and Ben sat up straight. So it hadn't just stopped at confiding in Aunt Esther.

"You what?" he demanded.

"I met Jack," she said, a smile in her voice. "And he's a wonderful boy. He looks so much like you. You said he looked like Sofia, but he's definitely a Blake."

"How, exactly, did you meet him?" he asked, his mind firmly on the conversation he'd had with Sofia about wanting to wait before any extra introductions. It was remotely possible that Sofia had changed her mind, but that was very remote. Once Sofia made her mind up about something, very little could derail her.

"I ran into them," his mother said with exaggerated casualness. "In the grocery store."

"Just ran into them?" he asked. "No premeditation there?"

"You make it sound like a crime," she retorted. "I happened to pass the McCray house the other day and noticed what car Sofia was driving. Then when I saw her car in the parking lot at the grocery store, I thought I would just pop in to buy some bread. There's no law against buying bread."

"Didn't say there was, but I told you that Sofia wanted to take this slow," he replied evenly. "I asked you to wait."

"I waited eight years," she retorted.

"No, you didn't. You waited a few days. You were oblivious the last eight years."

"Well, forgive me for caring!" she shot back.

Ben rubbed his hands over his eyes again and leaned his elbows onto his desk. "So tell me what happened."

"I saw him and I said hello. I introduced myself."

"How angry was Sofia?" he asked.

"She didn't seem exactly pleased, but there was no scene, if that's what you're worried about."

"I'm not worried about a scene, Ma." He heaved a sigh. She was being willfully obtuse about all of this and putting him in an incredibly awkward situation.

"Son, I'm sorry." Her tone turned contrite. "I know I should have waited. I promised you, and you know I'm not one to break my word. I actually only meant to look at him. I wasn't going to say a thing, but it kind of got away from me."

"Okay." He sighed. "So what did Sofia say?"

"She wanted me to wait." He was getting the truth now. He could hear it in her voice. "I didn't listen to her. I just got—" she sighed "—angry, I suppose. She never liked me much, and I felt pushed out. She's living with her father, so Jack gets to know her side of the family, but I'm told to wait on the outside and not let the child even know that I exist."

Her feelings had been hurt. She was being excluded from the one thing that mattered most to her—her family. When she'd lost her granddaughter, she'd grieved alongside Ben, and he could only imagine that the chance of being a grandmother again had awakened all those old feelings.

"I get that," he said. "I do understand, but do you really think I'd let that happen? Of course Jack will know his grandmother."

"Thank you."

"You've probably caused a whole heap of problems for me now," he said with a sigh. "Plus, you told Aunt Esther about Jack, too."

"She won't breathe a word."

"She already did."

There was a pause, and he could feel his mother's discomfort over the phone. "I'm sorry about that. I told her in the strictest confidence. I'm as angry as you are that she blabbed. She'll hear from me about this, you can be sure."

"What's done is done," he said. An argument between his mother and aunt wasn't going to take it back.

There was silence on the other end for a moment. "Can I see Jack again?"

"Eventually. First, I'm going to have to go smooth things over with Sofia."

Jack wasn't a prize to be passed around, and Sofia wasn't a woman to be discounted. While he knew that his mother had good intentions, he didn't exactly trust her patience.

"Ma," he said seriously. "I need you to promise me that you won't do this again. Keep your distance. Sofia needs time, and so does Jack."

"Jack was happy to meet me," she replied. "I gave him birthday money. He was thrilled."

"Yeah, well, Jack is a package deal with his mother. You should understand that."

She sighed. "I do."

"Good. I'll arrange something so that we can all get together. Soon. But don't waylay them again, okay?"

"Cross my heart."

"I'll talk to you later, Mom."

As Ben hung up the phone, he let out a frustrated grunt. It had probably been unrealistic to expect that he'd get any kind of privacy in a place this small, but he'd hoped it would last longer than this. Sofia was going to be upset. He could only hope that Jack wouldn't be overloaded with everything, and as for Steve...the poor guy was going through enough right now without family drama in the mix.

Yet somehow he could see his mother's point, too. She was being pushed to the sidelines when Sofia's father, whom Sofia had been estranged from for the past nine years, was right in the middle of things. She felt excluded when all she wanted to do was wrap her grandson in love.

He wished he couldn't see both sides quite so easily, because that meant that he didn't belong in either camp, and no-man's-land was a lonely place to be.

Ben looked at his watch. He might as well go home because tomorrow he was going to have to face the only woman he knew with a personality as strong as his mother's—Sofia.

Chapter Nine

"Why can't I keep it?" Jack asked plaintively.

Sofia and Jack sat together at the kitchen table, a bowl of cereal in front of each of them. Sofia's laptop was open beside her, her article about police presence in the lives of at-risk youth up on the screen. She was just doing one more pass through it before she emailed it to her editor.

"Because that's an awful lot of money for an eight-year-old." Sofia said. "Besides, I don't know if Shyla can afford that."

"But she gave it to me."

"Jack—" She shook her head. How to explain this in a way that wouldn't sound awful if he repeated it? She'd learned that lesson the hard way.

Morning sunlight streamed inside the window, warming the kitchen and making her father blink against the glare from where he stood at the counter. Food still wasn't appealing to

Steve this morning, and he was sipping a meal replacement shake.

"Just put it in a savings account," her father said. "And don't worry about Shyla. She won't starve."

Sofia dropped her spoon into the puddle of milk in the bottom of her bowl. Shyla had pushed her way in, and Jack was already enamored with the grandmother who had piled money into his hands. That would all be fine and good if that grandmother didn't actively dislike Sofia quite so much. It was ridiculous to think that someone could steal her son's affections from her, but tell that to her feelings.

"A savings account isn't a bad idea," she admitted. It would allow Jack to keep the money, while safely tucking it away somewhere out of sight for the next little while. Besides, eight wasn't too young to learn about saving for the future, was it?

There was a knock on the side door, and Sofia opened it to find Ben. He was in uniform, but his face looked older this morning—the lines deeper. He gave her a smile, and he stepped inside.

"How are you doing, Jack?" he said.

"I'm rich," Jack replied matter-of-factly.

"Yeah?" Ben raised his eyebrows. "How rich are you?"

"A hundred and twenty-one dollars rich," the

boy replied. "My new grandma gave it to me for my birthdays."

Sofia glanced at Ben in time to catch a pained look cross his face.

"We met her in the grocery store," Sofia said, biting back most of what she wanted to say about the encounter for Jack's benefit. Jack didn't need to carry around any guilt about this. He hadn't done anything wrong.

"Yeah." Ben's tone was also cautious, and he met Sofia's gaze apologetically. "She called me and said that...you'd met."

"So she's your mom?" Jack asked.

"Yes, she's my mom," Ben replied. "And she was really excited to meet you."

"So, what do I call her?" Jack asked. "I have a Grandma McCray. So is she Grandma Blake, then?"

"Sure, that would work," Ben said.

"She doesn't look much like a grandma to me," Jack said. "She doesn't dress like a grandma, and she doesn't have grandma hair."

Sofia winced, grateful that she'd been careful about what she said earlier. Jack had absolutely no discretion yet. She'd have to work on that with him. Ben didn't look daunted, however, and he laughed.

"She'd be thrilled to hear that," he said.

"Jack, can you go brush your teeth and make

your bed?" Sofia said. "The bus will be here soon, and you aren't ready to go."

Jack sauntered off toward the stairs, and her father glanced between Sofia and Ben. A beat of silence passed.

"I'm going to go have a rest in the living room," her father said with exaggerated nonchalance and headed out of the kitchen, muttering something under his breath. Once they were alone in the kitchen, she turned to Ben.

"Did you tell your mother that I wanted some space in dealing with this?"

"Of course, I did," he said. "She was just excited about having a grandson."

"Excited or not—" Sofia closed her eyes and heaved a sigh. She couldn't exactly explain that Shyla's dislike of her was more daunting than she cared to admit. "This isn't easy," she said at last. "It's getting more complicated by the day."

Ben crossed his arms over his chest and glared out the window for a moment. He sucked in a breath and looked back toward Sofia. "I can't control her, you know. She's a woman with her own mind."

"I know." Sofia grabbed the bowls off the table and brought them to the sink. "And Jack really likes her. That's a good thing, don't get me wrong. You said before that this would be harder on me, and I think that's what this comes down to. This *is* harder for me. Jack seems to be fine."

Sofia started rinsing the plates, letting the forks clatter into the sink. She hated admitting this and refused to look at Ben as she worked. It felt petty and a tiny bit spiteful to be so upset over a gift, but there were a lot of implications behind the gesture that gnawed away at her. It would be so much more comfortable to have a firm argument—that this was somehow terrible for Jack—but she didn't have that. All she had was her own discomfort.

"If your mom won't go along with a simple request for time," Sofia said, turning off the tap, "how can I trust that she'll back me up in my parenting? What happens when I draw a line, and Jack goes to his grandmother for sympathy?"

"That's jumping ahead," Ben replied. "We aren't there yet. Suffice it to say, I'd back you up."

"Would you?" Her father had never exactly backed up her mother. He'd been the fun one, and discipline wasn't part of his repertoire in parenting.

Ben leaned forward and fixed her with his dark gaze. She found herself holding her breath as he put his hands on her shoulders. He squeezed her gently, warm, strong hands holding her fast. "Sofia, I'll back you up. You can count on that, okay?"

She nodded, and he released her.

"So now that my mother has waylaid you in public, how do you want to do this?" he asked.

It was a good question, and Sofia went back to the table to grab the milk. She wasn't sure what the best course of action would be. Jack had met his grandmother, and he liked her. He wasn't going to just forget about her, and while Shyla did complicate things right now, meeting her was always part of the plan.

"I don't know," she admitted. "I like to feel in control of things, and right now, I don't."

"Yeah, I know that about you." He shot her a wry smile. "I have an idea. Why don't you and Jack come to my place for dinner? I'll invite my mom, too, and we can hash a few things out. We'll throw down some rules we can all agree on."

Sofia closed the fridge and stood in silence for a moment, weighing her options. Putting this off any longer wasn't really possible. Perhaps time in the same room together would let her and Shyla find some common ground. Sofia was no longer a teenager needing approval. She was a grown woman—a mother. Certainly Shyla could find something in her to respect if they had a chance to talk. And if they couldn't find some middle ground? She pulled her mind away from the precipice. The worst-case scenario wasn't helpful right now.

"All right," she said with a nod. "That is probably a good idea. When?"

"How about Saturday?" he asked. "I have the weekend off, and my mom could probably arrange for someone to cover her shift at the hotel."

This was moving faster than Sofia was comfortable with, but she also knew that she had caused this by waiting so long before telling Ben about his son. Shyla wanted to know her grandson, and Jack was now old enough to have a few desires of his own. He deserved to know his grandmother, and while Sofia felt pushed by all corners, she knew that her son was growing up. "Control" wasn't the most important thing here; it was a relationship.

"Saturday," she agreed.

"What can Jack eat?" Ben asked.

"Meat and potatoes, veggies, gravy if you use corn starch to thicken it. He's not really that hard to feed once you get the hang of it." She paused. "You do cook, right?"

"I can do meat and potatoes." He shot her a grin. "Yes, I cook. This will be nice, Sofia."

She wasn't convinced that it would be nice at all. It was necessary, though. She sent up a silent prayer that God would guide her. Being a mother was difficult enough without added tensions, and having Ben in her life again was proving to be more complicated than she'd ever imagined. Somehow the memory of him was easier to deal with than the reality. The memory of Ben didn't look straight into her eyes like that, warm her shoulders with his strong grip…and it certainly hadn't aged into this muscular cop before her. The memory had broken her heart all those years ago, but the Ben in front of her looked capable of even deeper heartbreak if she let her guard down too far.

Sofia knew her weaknesses, and one of those weaknesses was Benjamin Blake.

About fifteen minutes later, Ben was behind the wheel once more. Somehow his squad car made him feel more complete. It was like the flak jacket to his uniform—it protected him, made him stronger. Everyone needed something to buoy them up, and if a car could do that, it was easier than trying to find the person who could do that. Cars didn't up and leave you. And cars were replaceable.

Sofia's shoulders were higher than usual, and she stared out the window with a gaze intense enough to break glass.

"You okay?" he asked.

"Fine." She pulled a hand through her hair, letting the glossy tendrils fall back down around her shoulders.

"That's not true." He pulled away from the

curb and headed down the street. "You're stressed out."

"That's parenthood."

From what Ben had seen in his friends' lives, that was probably true. Balancing everything was tough, even in a two-parent home. Sofia had been doing this on her own for a long time.

"What are you worried about?" he asked.

"Oh..." She sighed. "I don't know. Everything. I work so hard to keep all of this balanced, and it doesn't take much to topple it."

"Maybe it won't topple." He slowed to a stop at an intersection and scanned the area with a practiced eye.

"You've obviously never dealt with an eight-year-old," she said with a sigh. Then she winced. "Oh, Ben, I'm sorry. I didn't mean anything by that."

"No, it's okay." It was true. He didn't have any parenting experience to speak of, and dancing around it wasn't going to change anything. "All I'm saying is that there are more adults in this situation than just you. You might have to let go a little bit and let other people love Jack, too."

"I can't just let go of my motherly duties," she said with a short laugh that told him she thought he was dead wrong. She reminded him a lot of his own mom when she talked like that. His mother had been pretty adamant about her job in protecting him, too.

"No, but you could let go of some of that worry," he said. "You call the shots with Jack—that's just the way things are—but we aren't working against you. We want Jack to grow up safe and secure, too, and he can't do that without his mom. Trust me on that. If there is one thing I'm very clear about, it's that Jack needs you."

She nodded slowly, her shoulders coming down ever so slightly. "Okay."

"I needed my mom when I was a kid," Ben said. "It's different as an adult, but I still need her in my life. She's my mom. It'll be the same for Jack. No one can ever take your place with him. I can guarantee you that."

"So I should relax," she said. What was it about Sofia that made her so beautiful when she was unsettled? It wasn't that he liked to see her this way, but when he got a glimpse of her beneath that self-controlled confidence, it softened him in a way he was never quite prepared for.

"You know, as much as you can." He shot her a teasing grin.

Sofia swatted his arm and laughed softly. "Are you calling me uptight?"

"I'm smarter than that," he replied with a low laugh. Any man his age who didn't see that trap coming was an idiot. He grew more serious. "You love hard, Sofia. There's no shame in that."

Sofia sank into silence, and they drove down some quiet, tree-lined streets. Most of the snow was melted now, except for some icy humps where snow drifts had solidified at the sides of the road during the lengthy prairie winter. Sofia had always been a passionate person, much like her mother. She felt things more deeply than others did, and when she loved, she loved with a rare abandon. He'd been fortunate enough to be on the receiving end of that love, even if he'd been unable to live up to it. The only problem he could see was that when she loved, she also took too much onto herself. Maybe that was an unfair judgment on a single mother, but she wasn't on her own. She had him. She just didn't see it.

Ben's cell phone rang, and he picked up the call on his hands-free device, the earbud in his ear keeping the conversation private.

"Hello?"

"Ben? This is Mom." Not Shyla, but Lisa's mother, Gwyneth Nichols. He glanced toward Sofia, then back to the road. He felt suddenly guilty.

"Hi, how are you doing?" he said.

"Not so good, actually," Gwyneth said. "Are you busy?"

"I'm, uh—" He glanced at Sofia again, and she returned his look with a curious rise of her eyebrows.

"There have been vandals, Ben," Gwyneth broke in, not waiting for his answer. Her voice shook with emotion.

"At your home?" he asked, frowning. The Nicholses lived in a good area. If vandals had managed to damage property there—

"No, no, at the graveyard. Lisa and Amanda's graves." She sniffled. "Ben, if you could just come and have a look, I'd feel better. It's not right having their resting places defaced like that."

The sear of anger effectively capped anything else that he might have been feeling. Letting go of Lisa and Mandy had been hard enough. The thought of anyone laying so much as a finger on their resting places... He glanced at his watch.

"I'll swing by the graveyard and then come talk to you. Are you at home now?" His voice was clipped and hard, and he wished he could soften it for Gwyneth's sake. She was sensitive, especially when it came to her daughter.

"Yes, we're home. Both of us." Gwyneth sounded slightly distant now, and he didn't know how to fix that. He'd just have to go take a look. He'd smooth things over when he could see her face-to-face.

"Okay, I'll see you in a little while," he said.

Ben hung up with a press of a button. Lisa's parents... Somehow, through all of this, he'd completely forgotten that he'd have to tell Lisa's parents about Jack. It was worse than having to explain it to Lisa, herself. Her mother had always thought the world of Ben. She'd told him that she'd been praying for him, Lisa's husband, from the time she was born. Lisa had seen the best in Ben, and so had Lisa's mother. Her father, on the other hand, had been a little harder to win over.

He glanced toward Sofia once more and caught her watching him, her brow furrowed.

"Your mom? Everything okay?"

"My in-laws." He grimaced. "Lisa's parents. Apparently, there's been some vandalism at the graveyard." He could hear the tension in his own voice, and he attempted to smile to cover it, but it didn't seem to work.

There was a beat of silence between them as Sofia's expression changed from curiosity to something he couldn't quite identify. She swallowed and looked away.

"Lisa's grave?" Sofia asked quietly.

"That's what they said. I'll have a look."

He couldn't guess at what Sofia was feeling sitting there beside him. She had a blank look on her face as if she were trying to hide it from him. Of course, he'd have to go look to see what had happened, but it felt wrong to be bringing Sofia with him, like an even deeper betrayal of what he and Lisa had had together than he'd already committed.

Ben pulled a U-turn and headed back toward the east side of town where the Shepherd's Rod Cemetery was located, one of the two cemeteries that served the town of Haggerston. The Shepherd's Rod Cemetery had once been outside of town, but the community had grown up around it, so that it was like a little garden between two subdivisions. As they neared the cemetery, Ben looked over at Sofia uncomfortably.

"You okay?" she asked.

"I want you to wait in the car," he said simply.

"You need some privacy," she concluded.

"Yes."

Sofia nodded, and he parked along the curb beside the wrought iron fence and the high gate. Sofia didn't move, but under her breath he heard her murmur, "Oh, my…"

"What?" He leaned forward and looked closer. Several graves within sight had been spray painted, brilliant blue lines swiped over them. The grass had similar treatment, and a kid was visible shaking a spray can in one hand. Blue streaks covered several gravestones. He couldn't see Lisa and Mandy's graves from this position, but he could see what the kid had done to others.

"Stay here," Ben growled, and got out of the car. His blood was boiling, and for the first time in a long time, he sent up an urgent prayer:

Lord, calm this anger. Don't let me regret what I do.

Chapter Ten

Ben plucked his radio from his belt and barked a quick message into the hand piece. "This is Delta Nine at the Shepherd's Rod Cemetery to investigate a ten twelve. I have a suspect within sight—"

Ben's training ran through his mind. There were protocols for everything, and those protocols kept him in step when his emotions demanded otherwise.

This isn't personal, he told himself firmly. It could be personal later, but not yet. Sofia got out of the car, too, and he shot her an incredulous look. What was it with the women in his life completely disregarding anything he said?

"What are you doing?" Ben demanded, keeping his voice low.

"This changes everything!" she retorted, nonplussed by his tone.

"What changes everything?" he hissed back.

"Your vandal is here. I'm reporting on this. Sorry, Ben, but I'm coming along."

Not having time to argue with her, Ben sighed and headed toward the gate. It hung partially open, and when he moved it, it let out a loud shriek. The kid looked up, and when he saw Ben, he exploded into a run.

"Of course," Ben muttered under his breath and broke into a run after him. His shoes thumped against the sodden grass, and he closed in quickly. He was in better shape than the kid gave him credit for, and he'd caught up with the boy by the time he reached the other side of the fence. He grabbed the kid's jacket and jerked him to a stop.

"What do you think you're doing?" Ben demanded. He spun the boy around to face him and was stunned to see Ethan gaping back at him. Ethan's eyes rolled around his head as he looked for an escape, and Ben heaved a sigh.

"Seriously?" he barked, releasing Ethan's jacket. "You're spray-painting graveyards now?"

Sofia's footfalls sounded softly behind him, and he glanced back as she caught up. Her hair was tousled by the wind, and she pulled a few strands away from her mouth where they'd stuck to her lip gloss. She was breathing hard, and her gaze swung from Ben to Ethan and back again.

"Don't we know you?" she asked with a frown, still huffing from the exertion.

"From the basketball court," Ben said, shaking his head. The anger seeped out of him, and he was left with a gutful of disappointment. He knew Ethan had some issues, but he'd honestly thought more of the kid than this.

"I didn't do it!" Ethan declared earnestly. "It wasn't me!"

The first thing that Ben had learned on the job was how quickly and effortlessly people lied. Everyone was innocent—framed, set up, in the wrong place at the wrong time—until you could point out all the proof against them.

"You're holding the spray can," Ben said, glancing around at the wet paint.

Ethan didn't answer, but he tossed the spray can to the grass beside him, as if that made a difference. Ethan rubbed his hands together and looked anywhere but at Ben.

"You realize this is a criminal offense, right?" Ben said.

Ethan was silent, and Ben looked over the boy's handiwork once more. It all looked angry—swipes and slashes, nothing artistic whatsoever. Normally taggers went for something that passed as art in some circles, but what Ethan had done was pure rage. There was more going on here. This wasn't just vandalism.

"Ethan," Ben said. "Why are you here?"

"Dunno."

"Yes, you do," Ben retorted. "I know you. You

aren't the kind of guy who does this. Not normally. So, what happened?"

"Gonna arrest me?" Ethan shot back, defiance flashing in his eyes.

"Not if you talk to me." Ben crossed his arms, refusing to take the boy's bait.

Ethan nodded toward a fresh grave several yards away. Ben glanced back at Sofia and caught her watching him, worry etched across her face. He sighed. He wasn't a baby chick. He didn't need mollycoddling. Obviously, he'd worried her, though, and he felt a twinge of guilt about that.

"Let's go take a look," he said, softening his tone.

Sofia walked next to him, and having her there was comforting somehow. The last time she'd been here had been at his grandfather's funeral, and they'd been dating at the time. She'd held his hand and stood in solemn silence next to him while he said farewell, but this time was different. Lisa's grave was here now. It changed things and made him a little guilty for appreciating the comfort of Sofia's presence.

Ben stopped at the headstone, his shoes sinking into the sod. Ethan stood next to him, his defiance gone. His shoulders slumped and he stared glumly at the freshly engraved words. Ben knew the name on the stone, and he looked at Ethan in concern.

"Your grandma died?" he said. "How did I not know this?"

Ethan dug his shoe into the grass. "I don't know."

Ethan had lived with his grandmother in the trailer park for years until they moved to a small basement apartment closer to Ethan's school. His grandmother had wanted better influences for Ethan, not that it had worked out that way. Ethan had been in trouble with drugs and truancy for the past couple of years. But if his grandmother was dead...

"Where do you live now?" he asked. "Are you back with your mom?"

"Nope. I'm crashing with a buddy."

That explained an awful lot, and Ben heaved a heavy sigh. Ethan was all but homeless at the tender age of fifteen, and no one in his life had noticed. Or perhaps he didn't have anyone left to notice.

"So why do this to her grave?" he asked.

"I dunno." Tears welled up in Ethan's eyes. He dashed a tear off his cheek with the back of one hand. Ben moved closer and put a hand on his shoulder, dipping his head to look into the boy's face.

"Your grandma loved you," Ben said. "She wouldn't have wanted this for you."

"Yeah, well she went and died," Ethan snapped.

Ethan was no different than any other kid—all wrapped up in his own pain. He thought that it all came down to his grandma dying, and while Ben's sympathy was with the boy, Ethan couldn't go around venting his emotions in criminal activity, either.

"Come here." Ben nodded in the direction of Lisa and Mandy's graves, and Ethan sullenly followed. Sofia stood back a little, the wind ruffling her hair around her face. Ben stopped at the familiar grave, a lump rising in his throat. A dried slash of blue dripped down the front. Obviously, Ethan had been here earlier. Lisa's name and dates were written across the stone, and underneath it all were the words, *More than anything*.

That's how much she'd always said that she loved him, and he'd recorded it on her gravestone as a kind of tribute to her. He might not have been all he should have been to Lisa, but Lisa had been amazing to everyone who knew her.

"You know who this is?" Ben asked, giving Ethan a long look. Ethan stared at the stone and shook his head.

"No."

"That's my wife." Ben crossed his arms over his chest. "And that—" He stepped to the left, to the tiny stone next to Lisa's. "That is my daughter."

"Oh, man…" Ethan backed away several steps. "Look, Officer Ben, I didn't know. If I'd known—"

"Every single stone here belongs to someone who was loved," Ben replied quietly. "You're angry. I get that. But the next time you're mad, come to me. I'll help you. You don't need to do—" he closed his eyes against the ugliness of it all "—this."

Ethan nodded, swallowing hard. "I'm sorry, man. Really sorry."

Sofia stood behind Ethan, her ankles pressed together and her hands folded in front of her. She watched them in silence, but despite her delicate appearance, there was strength emanating from inside of her. She was small, but she was steel strong.

"So where are you going to sleep tonight?" Ben asked.

"My buddy's place."

That wasn't a good answer, but Ben knew better than to argue it here. Ethan needed a place to stay with adult supervision. He needed to be brought to school, and he needed some drug rehab. That was a tall bill.

"Well, we're going to figure out something for you," Ben said. "Come back to the station with me."

Ethan froze, then took a step back. He bumped into Sofia and looked ready to bolt again.

"Am I under arrest?" Ethan asked cautiously.

"If that's what I need to do to get you back there," Ben shot back. "If you run, I *will* catch you."

Ethan cracked a small smile. "Fine, I'll come. No cuffs."

"Wouldn't dream of it."

Sofia waited until Ben was at her side before she turned and joined them in their walk toward the car. She slid a hand into the crook of Ben's arm—a gesture that he associated more with sympathy than anything else. He looked down at her, and for a split second, he saw the teenaged Sofia again, being his strength when he most needed it in the middle of a chilly graveyard. Ben glanced back at the graves that would be forever inside his heart, and then he picked up his radio and pushed the button.

"This is Officer Blake. The suspect has been apprehended, but I'm not pressing charges at this time. I'm bringing a minor into the station, and we need to contact Social Services." He paused, then pressed the button again. "And could someone order a pizza? The kid looks hungry."

He hung up his radio and pulled open the back door for Ethan to get in.

"In the back?" Ethan looked skeptical.

"I'm ordering pizza," Ben said with a shrug. "Doesn't count as an arrest if the officer gets you takeout."

Ethan sighed his acceptance and eased into the backseat. Ben met Sofia's gaze as he slammed the door shut. This was a tough day, no bones about it. Somehow, having Sofia here made it more bearable, but that comfort came with a barb: after dropping Ethan off with a social service agent, he'd have to go by the Nicholses' house and do some explaining of his own.

They drove back to the station where Ben, true to his word, set up Ethan with some pizza. A social service agent was waiting—a kindly older woman with a smile that transformed her face from plain to gorgeous. She took Ethan aside to talk with him in a private room away from the general hubbub of the office area, and while Ben sorted things out with them, Sofia settled herself at Ben's desk and took the opportunity to pull out her tablet and do some writing on a new article that she wanted to call *Sympathetic Policing*.

Sofia had to admit that Ben had a knack for this. She'd silently judged the fact that he hadn't enforced school attendance for these kids, but hearing Ethan's story reminded her that not every kid had a supportive home. Maybe Ben's more relaxed approach was better in the long run, getting kids like Ethan the fundamental care they so desperately needed when they were willing to accept it.

Not every kid had a mom who could care for him.

A half hour later, Ben came ambling over to his desk and cocked his head toward the exit. He shot her a small smile, his eyes warming as they met hers.

"Ready to go?" he asked.

"How's Ethan?" she asked.

"We're going to set him up with a temporary foster home," Ben said. "He'll get some counseling to help him deal with both his grief and the addiction issues."

"He's willing?" she asked.

"He wouldn't have been a week ago," Ben said. "But, yeah, he's willing. He knows he can't do all this on his own, and he trusts me enough now, I think."

"Are you pressing charges for the vandalism?" she asked, rising to her feet and tucking her tablet back into her bag.

"No, Ethan needs counseling, not a criminal record. I'll turn a blind eye this time. I've reported the vandalism to the cemetery. They'll start cleaning up."

Ben was kinder than she'd given him credit for. Having his wife's and daughter's graves desecrated would have been enough to throw the book at the kid for a lot of people, but Ben didn't seem to need that. He had something more—something deeper—holding him up. She could see his faith shining from deep down, and God had made a difference in his life.

"So, I need to head over to my in-laws' place," Ben said, his voice low. "I'll fill them in on what happened and put their minds at ease. This was pretty upsetting for them."

"And you'd like me to stay away for this part of it," she guessed.

Ben nodded, then pressed his lips together and met her gaze. He stepped closer to keep their words private, and the warmth from his arm emanated against hers. "Look, my in-laws will know about Jack soon enough, if they haven't heard already. My mom isn't exactly keeping this private. She's telling all her friends that she has a grandson, and well—" he shrugged "—it's better that they hear from me."

"Yes, that seems kinder," she agreed, and in spite of it all, she felt a lump rise in her throat. This wasn't her family, and she certainly didn't owe them anything, but they had her deepest sympathy. "I have some writing I need to get done, anyway."

"Okay. Well—" He nodded curtly, but he didn't make a move to leave. It was as if he were rooted to the ground beside her, and she had to stop herself from sliding a hand up his arm the way she used to years ago.

He's nervous, she realized in a rush. He was about to go tell his late wife's parents that he had another child—a child besides the little girl they'd all mourned together, and a child who would have broken their daughter's heart. She was the outsider to this—the one who came with the life-altering news. And he wasn't hers to comfort.

"Are you okay?" she asked instead.

"Yeah." He heaved a sigh. "I guess I'll see you tomorrow night for dinner at my place."

The dinner with his mother... She hadn't been looking forward to that dinner, but suddenly she could see that he needed this. He needed someone in this fractured family to get along, to hash things out. His shoulders just weren't broad enough to hold them all together.

"We'll be there."

"Let me give you a ride home," he said.

As they walked out of the station together, she wondered what was going on inside of him. His in-laws really loved him, and he seemed to love them, too. They'd all been blessed to have each other. It was the direct opposite of the family tensions they'd had as teenagers with her fighting parents and his protective mother. Ben had scored the jackpot with the Nicholses.

That's what it's supposed to be like, she thought sadly. But how many people really got that kind of relationship with the family they married into? Not many.

Lord, be with him. Be with them all.

Because the news of Jack was going to test all those relationships to the limit, she had no doubt.

Montana Twins For His Mother
Jolene thought also...
all those explanations to the issue...she was nel
thing.

Chapter Eleven

Saturday evening, Sofia sat on her old bed, listening to the sound of a news channel. She needed some time alone before they left for Ben's place—time to quiet herself, to reconnect with God—and so she'd set Jack up with some reading while her father watched the news. Jack was doing all right, considering all the changes he'd faced in the past couple of months. He'd moved from California to Montana, changed schools, reconnected with his grandfather, met his father, discovered a grandmother…

And while she wished this could stop at Ben's mother, now there were Lisa's parents, who would be affected by her presence, too. There were more people in the mix now—more tensions to navigate.

Sofia reached for her Bible and opened it to the book of Proverbs. She'd been reading a few verses from Proverbs each morning, and she had made her way to the sixteenth chapter. The second verse caught her eye:

All a man's ways seem innocent to him, but motives are weighed by the Lord.

It seemed to her that everyone in this situation was doing the right thing in their own eyes and hurting others in the process. There were too many currents for her to navigate on her own, and while she thought of herself as the wronged party, there were probably some people who thought otherwise.

I'm doing my best, Lord, she prayed. *Please, guide me. Help me to see what's best for Jack.*

Because this was about Jack. They were all scrambling, trampling each other's feet and offending each other in the process, but that didn't change that this was about her little boy. Part of her wanted to protect him from this mess, but she knew that she couldn't. This mess was his family, and without family, what did a boy have?

God would guide her—she had no other choice. Right now, she couldn't see the ladder, only the next rung, and that was this dinner at Ben's house.

Ben opened the oven a crack to check on the beef roast that had been broiling away for the past several hours. It smelled great, and he felt a surge of pride in this meal. He knew how to cook, but he didn't often entertain. When Lisa died, no one expected it of him anymore, and he'd let it go. It was easier than facing a house filled with sympathy.

Tonight, however, he wanted to do something for Sofia and Jack, something that showed them he could handle being a dad. Maybe, deep down, he wanted to do something to prove to himself he could handle this, too. He'd been all ready for fatherhood, or as ready as a man could be before Mandy was born, and he'd never been able to put any of those urges into practice. Now, he was launching into this eight years too late, and maybe it would help his confidence to do something dad-like...however "dad-like" looked. He'd never had a father of his own to learn from.

"It looks good," his mother said, peeking over his shoulder.

He shot his mother a smile. "So you're going to be nice, right?"

"I'm always nice."

"Yeah, yeah." She was nice, but she could be pretty strong-natured, too, and that was often misinterpreted for less-than-nice. He knew his mother's strengths, and he wasn't exactly blind to her weaknesses; he was just more understanding of them. She hadn't had an easy life, and some of those rough edges had been earned by some truly hard knocks.

Ben lived in one half of a duplex in a relatively new subdivision on the west end of town.

The kitchen was open concept and let him look right out the living room window without even a stretch. The cop in him liked the lack of corners. He relaxed more when he could see all the exits clearly. He'd been like that since he was a kid living in that trailer. Hearing the fights of couples in other thin-walled homes left him both tough-skinned and cautious. If he could see what was coming, he was pretty sure he could deal with it. He just didn't like surprises.

Like a son I didn't know about.

The doorbell rang, and before he could stop her, his mother went to answer it. She was only trying to be helpful, he knew. She'd always been the "my home is your home" kind of person, and she treated his place, and the rest of Haggerston, with the same attitude.

Sofia and Jack stepped inside, and Ben didn't miss the cool nod that passed between the two women. Jack seemed oblivious, which was just as well. Sofia wore a pair of close-fitting jeans and a pink turtleneck sweater that brought out the color in her cheeks. She looked fresh and youthful tonight. His mother was already doting over Jack, and Sofia looked back at her son uneasily as she came toward the kitchen.

"Hey," he said with a grin. "Make yourself comfortable."

His living room was furnished with a white fabric couch and matching love seat. Some floral pillows were piled to one side—Lisa's addition that he couldn't bear to change. A big-screen TV was turned off and hung like a void on one wall. A gas fireplace pumped some warmth into the room.

Sofia leaned against the counter and watched as he pulled the roast from the oven.

"This is a lovely home," she said.

"Thanks." The roast was nicely browned, and he put the whole pan onto the stove top, then stabbed the meat with a fork, hoisting it over to a cutting board.

"So how did things go yesterday?" Sofia asked. "With your in-laws, I mean."

"Better than I thought." His hands worked automatically, cutting the meat into thin slices while his mind went back to yesterday afternoon. Gwyneth had been more understanding than Ted, but the tension had been smothering. She'd asked a few questions about Jack and clarified the boy's age twice—obviously needing to be sure that he'd been born before Ben had met their daughter. Ted, on the other hand, had sat there in stoic silence. He still didn't know what the older man had been thinking, because Gwyneth had completely taken over the visit.

"It hasn't made things awkward for you?" she asked.

"Awkward, yes, but it'll be okay."

And it would be okay, eventually. Lisa had

obviously told her mother about his past with Sofia, and Gwyneth felt the pain in her absence.

Sofia didn't look as if she entirely believed him that all was well, but it felt like a betrayal to Lisa to explain how threatened by Sofia's memory his wife had felt deep down. He felt terrible for it, too, because he'd obviously done his job of husband rather poorly if his wife felt that way. It was more proof of his failure.

"You sure?" she asked. "I imagine it would be a pretty big surprise."

"Well…" He sighed. "It changes the story for them."

"I get that."

"I go from being the beloved son-in-law to the jerk who would have hurt their daughter, given enough time." Ben cut the last few pieces of roast, then transferred the meat from the cutting board to a platter.

"I have a feeling that Lisa wasn't as fragile as everyone thinks," Sofia said.

Ben eyed her in curiosity. She'd only heard about Lisa secondhand, but Sofia had always been intuitive.

"Why do you say that?" he asked.

"Because she married you, and you're no walk in the park," she said with a wry smile.

Ben laughed at that.

"She dealt with a difficult pregnancy, the demands of your job… Had things turned out differently, she would have dealt with all of this, too. In fact—" color rose in her cheeks "—I have a feeling I would have been the jealous one."

"I think you would have liked her," Ben said. "If you'd met her under different circumstances, that is. She was fun."

"I'm sure I would have." A smile touched her lips, and they exchanged a long look. Lisa would have liked Sofia, too. They would have sensed something good in each other—a shared resilience and love of life. But with his history with Sofia, they would have taken some time to get there.

Ben put the last of the meat onto the platter, then glanced back at his mother and son, who were talking in the living room. Shyla had brought a little photo album, and she'd been showing Jack some pictures of Ben as a boy.

"The food is ready to go," Ben called.

Shyla and Jack ambled over to the table, and Ben sucked in a deep breath, looking around at them. This was his family—a splintered group of people, tied together because of a boy they all loved.

"Have a seat," he said with a smile. "I made roast and potatoes, Jack. You should be able to eat that. Gravy is on the stove."

"I'll get it," Shyla said cheerfully.

"Mom, sit down," he said catching her arm as

she made a dash for the stove. She looked up at him, surprise registering on her face.

"I was just going to—"

"Just—" he heaved a sigh "—just have a seat, okay?"

He couldn't have his mother taking over in his home—not tonight, and maybe not again. She showed her love by taking charge, and while Lisa hadn't minded in the least, Sofia was different. Maybe Lisa would have been, too, after the baby. Motherhood seemed to change a lot of things.

Shyla went back to the table, shooting Ben an arch look. She was annoyed, he could tell, but he'd just have to live with that. Ben grabbed a bowl and a little ladle for the gravy made from the beef drippings on the stove top. When he came back to the table, they'd all taken their seats—Shyla and Sofia across the table from each other like a couple of opponents.

After the blessing, Ben passed the roast to Sofia, who served herself and Jack. His mother started on the potatoes, and there was the pleasant sound of cutlery clinking against plates. This was a start—a good start, he thought—toward building a few bridges here.

"This looks wonderful," Sofia said.

"This was how Lisa used to make the roast," his mother said. "And I taught him how to make the perfect mashed potatoes when he was Jack's age. So between Lisa and me, Ben was well cared for."

There was an awkward silence, then Ben said, "I'm not exactly a lost kitten, you know."

Sofia laughed uncomfortably, and his mother shot him a tight smile.

"Since we're all here together," Ben said, "I was hoping we could talk about a few ground rules."

"We don't need rules," his mother said. "We're family."

"We are family," Ben agreed, "but we're new at this. And there might be some hurt feelings—"

"I'm fine," his mother said quickly. "Don't worry about me."

"I think Ben was talking about me, actually," Sofia said, straightening her shoulders. Her gaze flickered toward Ben, then back to Shyla.

Shyla, who had been spooning potatoes onto her plate, froze with the spoon aloft. "Oh?" Her tone was just a smidge too chipper.

"I know that Jack really appreciates the birthday money you gave him, but from now on I need you to pass that kind of thing by me."

His mother regarded Sofia in silence for a moment, then she turned back to the potatoes, replacing the spoon in the bowl and passing them to Jack.

"I only meant to give him something special," she said after a moment.

"And it's appreciated," Sofia said, but her smile was tight, and she held her fork with a white-knuckled grip.

"You've had him to yourself for—" Shyla's tone turned sharp, and she stopped, closing her eyes and then opening them again in an obvious effort to regain her composure.

"I'm his *mother*," Sofia said. "You might not like me one little bit, but you can't just push me off to the side."

"Who's pushing you?" Shyla retorted. "If anyone has been pushed off, it's Lisa!"

"Lisa?" Tears shone in Sofia's eyes. "Lisa is the one person who will never be forgotten. She was loved—deeply loved. I know you all miss her, and I know that I'm not her—" Her voice broke, and she stabbed at a piece of meat, visibly trying to regain her composure.

If only Sofia knew that it had been the other way around. Sofia had been the one with a silent presence for the past nine years, the one impossible to compete with because of her very absence.

"This isn't about Lisa, Mom," Ben said. "No one is forgetting her, least of all Sofia. Trust me on that."

"Then what is it about?" Shyla demanded. "I haven't done anything wrong. I simply introduced myself to my grandson, since no one else thought it was necessary."

"I only asked for time," Sofia shot back. "That was all! Of course Jack was going to meet you, but I wanted to do this a little more slowly and carefully."

"Steve wasn't pushed away," Shyla retorted. "Jack knows his grandparents on your side. But I'm not welcome. Why not?"

For a moment, all was silent, and Ben could almost hear the hum of tension in the room. Jack looked from his mother to his grandmother, his eyes round.

"Because you hate me!" Sofia's fork dropped to her plate with a clatter. "I'm tired of dancing around this and pretending otherwise. You never did like me, and that hasn't changed!"

Shyla stared at Sofia, her mouth open as if she wanted to say something, then she snapped it shut.

"This is where you tell her that you don't hate her, Mom," Ben said quietly.

Shyla shot him a baleful glare. Silence descended upon the table, and for a few beats no one said anything. Even the forks were still. Sofia looked as if she might cry, and Jack's eyes were locked on his mother.

Shyla sucked in a breath. "I think perhaps we need to try a little harder at this, for Jack's sake."

Ben wasn't sure what he was expecting to-

night, but something had to give; something
had to soften. His mother swallowed a bite of
food, pink suffusing her cheeks. She was embarrassed.

"Yes, I think so, too," Sofia said, her voice
low. She reached over and brushed a curl away
from Jack's forehead. "I'm sorry, sweetie. I'm
fine."

Shyla put a hand on Ben's, then looked back
at Sofia.

"I know what it's like to love a little boy with
your whole heart," she said, her voice catching. "I started doing it twenty-six years ago. We
get protective. We try to shield them from what
might hurt them, and we act like mama bears
when we feel it's warranted."

Sofia blinked a couple of times but didn't
speak.

"I get it," Shyla went on, giving Ben's hand
a squeeze and then releasing him. "I probably
turned into a mama bear on you a few times
when it came to my Benjamin, but I don't hate
you. Far from it." She swallowed hard. "I won't
get between a mama bear and her cub, Sofia."
His mother shot him a tentative smile. "At least
not again. I'm sorry."

Ben knew how much that little speech had
cost his mom. She'd given up on winning this
one. She'd backed down. She'd let her righteous
indignation over how Sofia had handled all of

this go. That wouldn't have been easy for his mother, and Ben appreciated it more than she'd know.

"It's okay," Sofia said quietly. "And thank you, Shyla. I won't hurt your son again, either."

Sofia looked at Ben, and for a moment, their eyes locked. She'd been more magnanimous than he'd given her credit for. Sofia really was a good woman, and he found himself deeply grateful for both of these women in his life. They were strong, stubborn and fiercely protective—on the same side, they'd be unstoppable.

"So, Jack," Ben said, changing the subject. "Do you want to learn a few self-defense moves tonight?"

"Yeah!" Jack cracked a grin for the first time since sitting down at the table. "I want you to teach me how to throw a guy."

"Uh—" Ben glanced at Sofia again. They both smiled at the same time—a shared sense of relief, a shared sense of parenthood. "How about I teach you how to get a guy's hand off your shoulder if he grabs you?"

"Okay, maybe that, then."

The women weren't exactly chummy, but the icy atmosphere had melted, and they were regarding each other with something closer to friendliness. This was going to take time, but it was heading in the right direction. The first time he messed up royally and they were both angry at him, they'd solidify that hesitant relationship into something downright dangerous—a female alliance. And he wouldn't complain—not for a second.

Chapter Twelve

On Monday, Ben and Sofia were parked in the lot of Bernie's Burgers, one of the local greasy spoon joints that stuck to their winning recipes and didn't try to get fancy. A double bacon cheeseburger had hit the spot, and Ben pushed his burger wrapper into the take-out bag. It had been a long morning, and by the time lunchtime had come around, both he and Sofia had been starving.

They had both been subdued all morning. This would be their last official day of riding together. Sofia was supposed to be with him for a full two weeks, but her editor had cut the assignment short when another journalist had to leave unexpectedly for a family emergency.

"So this is our last lunch together," Ben said, trying to keep his tone light.

"Not our last one. Don't make it sound so

final." She adjusted her last bite of burger in the wrapper she held.

"You saying you'll grab a bite with me sometime?" he asked hopefully.

"Of course." Her sad smile betrayed her feelings underneath. She'd miss him, too. But they were still Jack's parents, and he knew he'd see more of her. There would be birthdays and holidays, school functions... Just not every day. He'd miss this daily time together, but it wouldn't do to dwell on what he couldn't change.

Ben wiped his mouth with a napkin and changed the subject. "It looks like social services has located Ethan's mother."

"Where was she?" Sofia asked past a bite of burger in her cheek.

"She was over in Ellison." Ellison was the same size as Haggerston and about forty miles away.

"Why so far?" Sofia asked.

"She's been in drug rehab, and they have a rural facility out there. She and Ethan's grandmother hadn't been on good terms, so she kept her distance. I don't know all the details. I do know that counselors will try to mediate something between mother and son."

"Will she be able to take him back in?" Sofia asked with a frown.

"It's hard to tell. These things can get complicated." He sighed. "You know, when I started out in this career I liked the whole black-and-white concept. There was right and there was wrong. There were laws to be maintained."

"I find that hard to imagine." She smiled.

"Nice clear lines are pretty comforting when you're trying to put your own life back together." His mind went back to those days after Sofia had left, when he was left with his own life and his own mistakes, and he had to make some choices. He'd known he wanted a better life than the one he'd been leading, and that was what brought him to church the first time. He wanted answers, and he wanted something he could feel. He wanted black and white, he just didn't get it very often.

"There don't seem to be many clear lines with Ethan's situation," Sofia said quietly, crumpling her own wrapper and shoving it into the bag after his.

"There aren't in most." Ben started the car again, and he pulled out of the parking spot and headed toward the street. His cell phone rang just as he turned on to Main Street, and Ben glanced at the number before picking the call up on his headset. It was Mavis.

"Officer Blake? Officer Blake?" Mavis didn't even wait to hear his voice. She sounded panicked, and something crashed behind her. "Help me! He's doing it again!"

Ben slapped on his siren, and the few cars on

the road eased slowly to the side to allow him to pull a screeching U-turn. He stepped on the gas, all before answering her.

"On my way, Mavis. What's going on?"

There was a shout on the other end, then the line went dead. Ben's heart dropped into his stomach. It always took a few seconds for his training to kick in and take over, and he glanced at Sofia as he slowed just enough to make a corner.

"What's going on?" Sofia gasped, grabbing at the side of the door as he whipped around the corner.

"That was Mavis. It sounds like Mike is beating her again."

Sofia didn't answer, and when he next glanced in her direction, she was blanched, eyes wide and lips pale. He didn't have time to comfort Sofia, and he hoped he wouldn't have to—not yet.

"Watch out!"

"It's under control, babe," he said, easing around a cyclist and picking up speed again. He realized belatedly the endearment he'd used— one from their dating days—and he grimaced. Last night, as he lay in bed thinking about how Sofia and his mother seemed to have started to reconcile their differences, he realized that the most challenging part of co-parenting with Sofia wasn't going to be balancing family members.

It was going to be walking that line between friendship and something more. He might have learned to appreciate the gray area in his job, but he was still the kind of guy who was all or nothing when it came to his heart, and raising a boy with a woman who made him feel the way he did, and keeping this properly balanced… that was the hard part. It would only get harder.

I'll have to get tougher. It seemed like the only solution.

They'd be there any minute now. He picked up the radio and barked in a quick status update. He could handle this one on his own, but backup never hurt. He also suspected that they'd need an ambulance, even if Mavis wasn't badly hurt. He wanted to get medical evidence this time—proof of what her husband was doing to her.

The Raven Hill subdivision was quiet this time of day, and as Ben whipped up the road toward Butternut Drive, he sent up a prayer that they'd be in time…and that Mavis had managed to stay far enough away from Mike to keep safe.

"I'm going in first," Ben said. "You can come with me, but stay back. Understand?"

"Yes." Sofia sucked in a deep breath and leaned forward as they made the last turn. Her tone was even, and she was physically bracing herself for the turns now. He found himself impressed with her recovery over the past couple of minutes. There was color in her face again—adrenaline had taken over.

Good. She'd need that. He had no idea what they'd find when they arrived.

Ben screeched to a stop in front of the house and was out of the car in a matter of seconds. With one hand on his gun in his belt, he went around the side of the house. He could hear Sofia's breath close behind. He put a hand back as he stopped at the side door, and she ran into it, the softness of her jacket and stomach colliding with his hand before she backed up.

Ben lifted a finger, and she nodded quickly.

"Police! Open up!" Ben barked, and without waiting for a response, he tried the knob. It was open. Ben stepped inside, his instincts tingling, waiting for an attack. The sound of clatter and thumps came from deeper inside the house, and he led the way through the kitchen and toward the hallway.

There was a scream, and Mavis came flying out of the bedroom, her eyes rolling in panic. Her top was torn, and there was a trickle of blood coming out of her nose. When she saw Ben, she lurched in his direction, Mike right behind her. Ben stepped aside and let Mavis go past him toward Sofia, then closed the gap with his solid body. Sofia could take care of Mavis, he had no doubt. His focus was on Mike—and Mike was not getting through him.

Mike stood in the hallway, shirtless. His fists were clenched at his sides, and he was breathing noisily through flared nostrils. Mike seemed to assess the situation pretty quickly, because he immediately put up his hands in submission. Ben was mildly disappointed. He would have enjoyed an excuse to use some extra force in cuffing him.

"What's going on here?" Ben asked, his voice low and controlled.

"Nothing, nothing…" Mike shook his head. "Just a little disagreement. It might have gotten a little loud." Mike pasted a smile on his face and slowly lowered his hands. "We're okay. Aren't we, Mavis?" His voice held an order.

Ben glanced quickly back. Sofia had an arm firmly around Mavis's shoulders. A red welt was forming on one side of Mavis's face, and her nose looked swollen. She cradled her casted wrist in the other hand, and her wild eyes were fixed on her husband.

"So who hit her, then?" Ben asked.

"That was an accident. She fell."

That was a blatant lie, the kind that made Ben's stomach sour. Why was it that invertebrates like Mike denied the very thing that made them feel the most manly behind closed doors?

"Is that true?" Ben said, looking back again. He wanted her to contradict him, to stand up and say what happened. It would help immensely in prosecution.

"Yes." Mavis's voice trembled. "I fell in the bedroom. I hit my face against the dresser."

"Mavis…" Softening his tone took effort, especially when his adrenaline was pounding like this, but he didn't want to scare Mavis more than she was. She was following her husband's lead, though.

"It's true," Mavis insisted. "Mike didn't lay a hand on me."

That was an outright lie. Mavis knew as well as Mike did that one more domestic violence episode and Mike would be spending some time behind bars. It would be a lot more effective, though, if they could get Mavis to write a reliable statement.

"You just tripped and fell against the dresser?" Ben said, shaking his head. "Come on, Mavis. We both know that isn't what happened. Did he push you? Or was that with his fist?"

Mavis shook her head adamantly, then winced in pain at the sudden movement. "Neither. I just stumbled."

Ben met Sofia's gaze, and they exchanged a solemn look. Mavis was scared, that much was clear.

"Why don't you sit with Sofia in the kitchen?" Ben said gently. "I'll take care of things here with Mike."

Sofia nodded and nudged Mavis back down the hall. The older woman leaned against her, and Sofia slid an arm around Mavis's waist in order to better support her weight. Sofia was good at this, Ben realized. Many women would have been a crying mess at this point, having witnessed a frightening episode of violence, but Sofia was more than holding it together; she was holding Mavis together, too.

When the women disappeared around the corner, Ben turned to Mike, pulling his cuffs from his belt.

"She called for help, Mike," Ben said, his tone carefully controlled. "We can use that as evidence in court. Plus, we'll have a doctor's report for her current injuries."

"She doesn't have any injuries," Mike said. "I barely touched her."

"So you admit that you did?" Ben asked evenly.

"No! I don't admit to anything." Mike scowled, and Ben whipped him around and slapped the cuffs onto his wrists. "I want my lawyer."

"I'm sure you do," Ben muttered. Mike was a coward. He'd beat his wife in private and plead for leniency in public. His wife would back him up.

No woman provoked that. No woman asked to be beaten. Ben didn't care what a woman did; if a man lifted his hand against her, he was solidly in the wrong, and Ben would throw all the weight of the law behind him in making sure that the perpetrator was punished. This was where he was a little less inclined toward the gray area.

Ben knocked Mike in the middle of his back to get him moving toward the front door. "Mike Layton, you are under arrest. Anything you say can and will be used against you in a court of law. You have the right to an attorney..."

"I *said* I wanted an attorney."

"Shut up." Ben pulled open the front door where two cruisers were already waiting. He felt some of the adrenaline starting to seep away. "If you can't afford one, one will be appointed to you. Do you understand these rights as they have been explained to you?"

Let these charges stick, Ben prayed, *so that he can never lay a finger on that woman again.*

Sofia filled the white, plastic kettle and plugged it in. She grabbed a couple of cookies from a cellophane package on the counter and put them on a plate in front of the shaken woman. Mavis didn't even look at them.

"Are you okay?" Sofia asked quietly. It was a ridiculous question, she knew. Mavis was most certainly not okay—her fingers trembled, and her face was puffy and red where bruises were already starting to darken.

"What will he do to Mike?" Mavis asked suddenly, looking back toward the hallway.

"He's just detaining him," Sofia said gently. "He'll need to ask a few questions."

Was it wrong of her to hope that Ben was less than gentle in that questioning? She sent up a prayer for God's guidance. She had no idea how to help this woman. Mavis was up against more than Sofia could even imagine.

"I won't testify against him!" Mavis declared, pushing the cookies aside.

Sofia sank into the chair opposite her. The front door opened and shut. From her position at the table, she could see just out the living room window where the red-and-blue lights from cruisers flashed.

"It's getting worse, isn't it?" Sofia asked quietly. "His rages, I mean. I think you felt like you had a handle on this before, but it's slipping out of control."

"I don't know what you're talking about."

Mavis stared stubbornly at the fridge as if that would make all of this go away, and Sofia could understand that wish. Mike seemed to keep her bouncing from one extreme to the other, and what woman wouldn't wish away that kind of misery? If only wishes were enough. Even prayer wasn't enough this time. Mavis had to make a choice to walk away—that was the only thing that would stop Mike.

The front door opened and shut again, and after a moment, Ben came into the kitchen. His height and broad shoulders seemed to fill the room, and Mavis stared up at him, looking daunted. Ben exchanged a look with Sofia, then he squatted in front of Mavis, looking at her seriously.

"Where is my husband?" Mavis asked archly, but her hands were still trembling.

"He's being taken to the station," he said quietly. "He's being charged with domestic violence."

"But I'm not pressing charges!" Mavis said.

"You don't need to," Ben said gently. "The prosecutor can proceed with the case without your testimony. The charges are already laid."

Tears welled up in Mavis's eyes, and she looked imploringly at Sofia as if Sofia could somehow change all of this.

"But I love him..." Mavis whispered, and Sofia's heart ached at those words. She had no doubt that Mavis loved her husband, but it didn't change what her husband had been doing to her. Mavis needed help—more than Sofia or even Ben could provide.

"Do you understand what I've told you?" Ben asked.

Mavis nodded, and Ben rose to his feet. His

hand brushed across Sofia's shoulder in a whisper of comfort.

"The ambulance is here," Ben said. The side door opened, and an officer gestured two EMTs inside. "They'll take you to the hospital to make sure that you're okay. I imagine you're in quite a bit of pain right now."

"I'm fine," Mavis said firmly. "I'm not in any pain."

"When the shock wears off, you will be." Sympathy suffused Ben's face. "Let the doctors help you." Mavis looked ready to argue, when a different look crossed Ben's face. It was a look of pleading. "For me, Mavis. Please."

Mavis was still for a moment, then nodded. "I'll go."

The EMTs wasted no time in helping her to her feet. Sofia could see more than the facial bruises. Mavis was favoring her broken wrist—probably reinjured, she guessed—and she limped heavily. When they'd left the house, her energy drained away, and she looked toward Ben.

"Just give me five minutes alone with that man," Sofia said through gritted teeth.

"You and me both." He sighed. "Come on. Another team is going to comb this place for evidence."

The house was suddenly filled with uniforms, and as they walked out the front door, Sofia blinked in the welcoming sunlight. The ambulance was just pulling out, lights flashing, and she watched it go with a rush of relief. Having Mavis taken to the hospital seemed to end this episode.

"You doing okay?" Ben's voice was low and close to her ear. Sofia looked up and shook her head.

"I'm okay. Wow... I don't know how you do that."

"At least I can come and break it up and press charges," Ben replied, pulling open the passenger-side door to his cruiser. "If I didn't have this job, there wouldn't be much I could do to fix it. That would be worse."

Sofia entered the car, and when Ben got into the driver's side, he looked over at her. His dark eyes seemed to hold all sorts of suppressed emotions, and he pulled a hand through his short dark hair.

"Talk about going out with a bang," Sofia said quietly. "It's a memorable last day, isn't it?"

"That's one way to put it." His tone was low and deep. "You impressed me today, Sofia."

"Did I?" She raised her brows. "How?"

He started the car, then reached over and gave her hand a squeeze. "I wasn't sure if you'd crack in there."

Sofia attempted to smile but didn't think she succeeded. She'd been surprised at her own strength in there, too, but that strength was now seeping away, leaving her shaken. Ben hadn't taken his hand away, and he moved his fingers slowly over hers in gentle circles.

"I'm sorry," she whispered past the lump in her throat. "Speaking of cracking..."

When she raised her misty eyes to look at him, she found his gentle gaze locked on her face. He released her fingers and wiped a tear from her cheek with one rough thumb. She leaned her face into his hand, finding comfort in his gentle touch. It had been a long time since she'd had a man's strength to lean against, and it felt much better than she even cared to admit. He didn't pull back, and when she sucked in a breath to say something, he moved closer.

Sofia didn't say anything more, and he moved nearer again, this time closing the distance between them as he pressed his warm lips against hers. She let her eyes fall closed and leaned forward into his kiss.

For a moment, everything was a warm darkness around them. The softness of his lips and the whisper of his breath against her face made her forget about everything else. Then he pulled away, and her eyes fluttered open again.

"Oh..." she murmured. Had she just kissed Ben Blake? Was she going to regret this later?

"Sorry." A smile tugged at one corner of his

lips, and in this warm, close moment, he didn't look sorry at all.

"It's okay," she said, her voice trembling slightly. She licked her lips and looked out the window. No one seemed to have noticed them.

"I'll take you home," Ben said, clearing his throat. "I've got a bunch of paperwork for this arrest to do, anyway."

He signaled, then eased away from the curb, and Sofia leaned her head back. The memory of Ben's lips on hers was still strong in her mind, and it reminded her of kisses shared all those years ago when everything seemed possible and loving each other was the only thing they thought mattered.

But they were older now, and so many other things mattered, too. She just needed to get her head clear again so that she could remember them.

Chapter Thirteen

The next morning, Sofia received a call from the doctor's office requesting that her father come in immediately. Being summoned for an unscheduled visit wasn't a good sign, was it? Doctors didn't bring you in to congratulate you on having admirable lymph nodes or an exceptional spleen. So she got Jack onto the school bus, told Ben she was taking a morning off and drove her father to the doctor's office. After a few minutes, they were ushered into an examination room, and they sat uncomfortably in the quiet.

Her mind had been on that kiss with Ben since it had happened—the memory of his lips on hers, the warmth—but with that phone call had come an extra reminder of reality. Life wasn't just about the warm kisses, it was about being able to trust a man to be there for the hard times, too—to *stay.* Life was full of surprises—not all of them pleasant.

"It'll be fine," her father said, glancing in her direction.

"Of course it will be."

She hoped she sounded more reassuring than she felt. She sucked in a breath and looked down at the fashion magazine on her lap, showing glossy photos of impossibly thin women looking defiantly into the camera. She flipped it shut. The room was small and the walls thin. She could hear the murmur of voices in the next room over, and she wondered how long that person's appointment would take before the doctor would come talk to them.

"How have you been feeling?" Sofia asked.

"Terrible." Her father smiled wanly. "Isn't that what chemo is all about?"

Maybe it was. She nodded. "Maybe this visit has to do with that thing they stuck in your arm." She nodded toward the PICC site where a tube emerged from her father's arm, solidly taped down so that it wouldn't move around, but even so, there was bruising.

The door opened, and a doctor stepped inside. He was an older man with tanned skin and dark brown hair. His white coat was pushed aside, and two pens poked out of a pocket. He looked at the chart, then up at her father, his expression serious. "Hello, Steven."

"Hi, Doc."

The doctor looked toward Sofia, giving her a polite nod. She recognized him from that first appointment she'd been to with her father. The doctor sat down on the stool in front of him. He reached forward and felt her father's neck with slow hands, then turned over his arm to look at the PICC.

"So, what's the problem?" Sofia asked. "It sounded like there was an issue when your office called this morning."

"There is an issue," the doctor said. "With your father's history with alcohol, I took the liberty of ordering a few extra tests, and they came back positive for alcohol in his blood."

"What?" Sofia looked at her father in surprise. "You told us before that he wasn't supposed to have any alcohol during this treatment."

"Even so," the doctor replied, looking back at his clipboard. "Blood tests don't lie. However, that doesn't mean that Steven has been drinking. It's possible the chemotherapy could be skewing our results. All the same, we should look into it. We could do a liver panel and see what it shows us, and I would recommend a CAT scan just to be sure…"

The doctor's words flowed over her, and Sofia's mind whirled with possibilities. Was her father sicker than they thought? Were there other issues that would put off the chemotherapy?

"Stop. You don't need more tests," Steve said, huffing out a sigh. "Look, I just needed to relax a bit. That's all."

Sofia stared at her father in surprise. Cancer was nothing to toy with. Would he seriously risk his recovery by drinking during his treatment? Maybe she shouldn't be surprised, after all. He'd always made his own rules, so why not now?

"When did you do this?" she asked. "Not when you were with Jack—"

"No, of course not. When I took a walk."

Sofia's mind went back to those evening strolls her father liked to take, and she wondered where he'd stashed the alcohol that he'd taken with him. To think she hadn't noticed—that was almost embarrassing. What kind of a parent was she going to be when Jack was a teenager if her father could go out, drink and come back without raising her suspicions? But she wasn't supposed to be parenting her father. That was the difference.

"I told you before what alcohol would do when mixed with these medications," the doctor said. "Do I need to go over that again with you?"

"No." Steve looked away. "I'm sorry. I'll stop."

"You'd better." The doctor rose to his feet and tore a slip from a pad. "This is a prescription for an anxiety medication that won't affect your chemotherapy. It will help you relax. Leave the booze alone."

"Thank you, Doctor," Sofia said quietly, and she waited until the doctor had left the room before she turned to her father. "I can't believe you'd do that, Dad."

Her father rolled his eyes. "I'm fine."

"You won't be if this chemotherapy doesn't do its job!" she retorted. "What were you thinking?"

"I was thinking I wanted a few blessed minutes to myself!" he shot back. "My house is full of people now!"

Were they more underfoot than she realized? Her father had been living alone in that house for the past nine years, and maybe filling it back up again wasn't as pleasant a prospect for him as she'd hoped it would be.

"If you don't want us living with you right now—"

"No." Steve shook his head. "That's not what I said. You're more than welcome—"

"I don't need a favor!" Sofia cut in, struggling to keep her tone low enough so that what they said wouldn't travel through the thin walls. "I thought I was helping *you*."

"You are."

"So why are you sneaking off to drink, then?"

"I told you," he said gruffly. "To relax. Having cancer is a bit stressful, if you hadn't noticed."

Sofia fell silent. Yes, having this illness would be frightening, and he had her full sympathy there. There were probably stresses that she hadn't even thought of yet.

"Here's the thing, Dad," she said, rising to her feet. "I came back because I wanted a relationship with you. I wanted to make up for the last nine years, and I want to try—" A lump in her throat choked her voice.

"Now, now…" Her father cleared his throat. "It was a few nips now and again. Not the end of the world. Doctors tend to exaggerate—"

"They don't!" she snapped. "And you'd better start caring a little more about the length of your life, because I'm not ready to lose you yet!"

Her father blinked. "Okay. Got it."

Sofia put a hand under her father's arm as he rose to his feet. He was thinner than before, and there were dark rings under his eyes now where there hadn't been before. He might not have been a stellar father, but he was her father, and if she lost her chance at a relationship with him, she'd never forgive herself for the time she wouldn't get back.

She handed him his jacket. "Now, let's get you home."

* * *

That evening, Ben cruised slowly down a side street. The sun had set in an explosion of red that bled slowly away until all that was left was a crimson ribbon along the horizon. The wind was warm tonight, and he'd opened his window a couple of inches to let in some fresh air. He liked this part of the job—the quiet, the driving, the solitude. That was what he'd liked about his motorcycle, too.

Should he get himself another one? Sometimes he thought he might. He'd gotten rid of his last one when Lisa got pregnant. It just didn't seem practical anymore. But things were different now, and he was alone again. Maybe a gorgeous chrome and black bike would fill some of that void.

Ben had been beating himself up all day for that kiss the day before. He'd thought that if he'd avoided being alone with Sofia on a dusky porch that he'd be safe, but apparently in the middle of the day in his squad car hadn't been all that safe, either.

What was I thinking?

Why had he let himself do that? It wasn't as though she'd been asking to be kissed and he obliged... This was squarely on him. He was the one who kissed her, and the fact that she'd kissed him back wasn't the point.

But she *had* kissed him back.

Ben tried to push away the memory of her dewy eyes and the way her pink lips had parted the tiniest bit before he gave up on holding back. She'd leaned into his lips, and if he'd had a little more room, he would have pulled her close against his chest and been a little more thorough about it.

"Idiot," he muttered aloud. He wouldn't blame her if she didn't want to ride with him anymore now, and maybe that was for the best. He still felt things for her that he shouldn't be feeling. That all belonged in the past, and it just kept pressing forward, no matter how much he reasoned with his emotions.

As if having fathered a child with her wasn't enough, now he was going back to old patterns. Nine years had passed. He'd had time to fall in love again, get married, have his heart torn out—that was enough time to get over a high school girlfriend! So why wasn't time on his side?

Lord, I'm sorry for having kissed her. It was wrong of me. The worst part is, if I were sitting in the car with her now, I would kiss her again. What does that make me?

There was no point in trying to hide his true feelings from God, and it felt good to articulate it to the One who could actually help him. Except no matter how much he pleaded, God hadn't taken away these feelings for Sofia. Why was God making him fight this one alone?

As Ben came up to a four-way stop, he slowed. Another car was coming toward him, and it wasn't slowing. It swerved slightly, weaving close to the center line, then away again before it hurtled past the stop sign. Ben put on his siren and spun a U-turn, taking off after the car.

At least stopping a speeder would get his mind off of things. He stepped on the gas. The car wasn't stopping, even with a siren on its bumper, and Ben picked up his radio.

"This is Delta Nine. I've got a suspected 10-55 on Willoughby Way, eastbound."

The car started to slow, and Ben followed it as it turned down another street lined with older houses, the car creeping along until it finally came to a stop. Streetlights illuminated the area, and Ben punched the license plate number into the computer on his dash, waiting a moment until the information popped up on his screen.

Steven McCray. He heaved a sigh.

"This is Delta Nine. I've got the suspect stopped on Beaver Road, just North of Willoughby. I'm going to investigate."

He pushed open his door and stepped out. Unsheathing his flashlight, he turned it on and scanned the area before approaching the driver's side of the vehicle. He shone the light down into the car, and Steve blinked and tried to shade his eyes. After a moment, he unrolled the window, and the smell of booze wafted out.

"Hey, Steve," Ben said cordially. "Care to step out of the vehicle?"

"Just on my way home," Steve said, his words slightly slurred.

"Step outside, Steve."

Ben opened the door for him, and Steve took a moment to get his balance before getting out of the car. He swayed slightly, looking at Ben with bloodshot eyes.

"Drinking tonight?" Ben asked. It was a silly question, but one they always asked.

"No. No, sir." Steve shook his head. "Just out for a drive."

It was a sign of exactly how intoxicated Steve was that he tried to lie about it, and Ben found sadness welling up inside him. Somehow the pathetic lie only made this harder. He didn't want to have to do this tonight. Ben pulled out his Breathalyzer.

"I need you to blow here."

"Really?" Steve took an unsteady step backward. "Is that really necessary?"

"Afraid so. Blow here, please."

Steve complied, and the test proved what Ben already knew. He pulled out his cuffs.

"Turn around, Steve."

The older man complied, and Ben put on the cuffs, being as gentle as possible in the process.

He patted Steve on the shoulder, then reached into the car to retrieve Steve's keys and swung the door shut.

"What's this about?" Steve demanded slowly, his tongue not working properly around the words.

"It's about drinking and driving," Ben said evenly. "Come on. You'll come with me to the station to sober up."

This wasn't the first time that Ben had intervened because of Steve's drinking, but he wouldn't be able to cut any corners. When a man got behind the wheel he was no longer just a threat to himself, he was a threat to everyone on the road.

"Hey," Steve whispered loudly, leaning in closer so that his beer-laden breath heaved directly into Ben's face. "Whatever you do, don't tell my daughter about this one. She'll be really mad."

"Let's go."

He didn't want to be the one arresting Steve tonight. It would have been better that someone else catch him. Let another cop take responsibility for hauling him into the station and Ben wouldn't have to be the one to tell Sofia the difficult truth.

But maybe it was better she heard it from him. Maybe it would be easier for her. She'd missed a lot in the past nine years, and her father's steady downward spiral was one of them. This would hurt her, and sometimes this kind of news could be gentler from a friend...even if it was much more difficult for him.

Chapter Fourteen

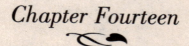

Sofia looked at her watch. It was nearly eleven o'clock, and her father still wasn't home. If he weren't weakened from his treatments, she wouldn't worry—he was a grown man, after all. He had friends. Maybe he even had a girl-friend that she didn't know about. It wasn't as if she'd kept up with the details of her father's life, and he certainly didn't owe her an accounting of his time.

Sofia opened the cupboard and looked inside. There were cans of soup, some microwave pop-corn, a bag of gluten-free, dairy-free, taste-free cookies...

Oh, Jack...if only you knew how many calories you saved me from.

Then she remembered the cookie dough in the back of the freezer, and went in search of it. Scratch the rescue from extra calories. When she worried, she ate. She'd always been that way, exactly like her mother. Sofia remembered her mother staying up late all those years ago. Sofia was supposed to be sleeping, but she'd creep to the top of the staircase and look down at her mother's worried, wan expression as she paced around downstairs.

"Go back to bed," her mother would say with that hint of an Italian accent, even after all those years in America. "I'm just cleaning up a little before I turn in, too."

But her mother hadn't been simply tidying up a little, she'd been waiting up. Even back then, Sofia knew the difference. Her mother had taken care of the home, worried over the bills, raised Sofia and still had to stay up pacing in hope that Steve would show up soon. She could only imagine the scenarios going through her mother's mind.

When Steve did show up, thumping up the side steps and singing loudly as he stumbled into the kitchen, that was when the arguing would start. Sofia's mother would confront him with her worries. He would tell her that he was his own man. Her mother would get angrier and angrier until she just started hollering at him in Italian. That's when her father would say those barbed words: "If you hadn't been pregnant, Valentina... If you hadn't been pregnant already—" They'd argue, and her father would sleep in the La-Z-Boy chair downstairs, and her mother would stomp up to bed where Sofia could remember hearing her crying softly by herself.

Some marriage. Sofia sighed. *I'd rather be alone than deal with that...*

Sofia could sense the irony that she'd stepped into her mother's shoes tonight, staying up worrying over her father. It was a lonely feeling, and several times this evening she'd been tempted to pick up the phone and call Ben—it would be comforting to hear his voice—but she stopped herself.

Not now... She couldn't allow herself to lean on Ben now. She was worried and stressed out. It would be *too* comforting, and these were the times she needed to hold herself up. After that kiss in his car, she knew that he felt the same attraction that she'd been feeling, and she needed to be careful. When she closed her eyes she still could feel the softness of his lips against hers—

Sofia peeled back the wrapper on the cookie dough tube and took a small bite. Some mothers hid stashes of chocolate. Apparently, she had raw cookie dough in the back of the freezer. Chocolate was probably a better idea.

She wandered into the living room and turned on the TV. There was a rerun of some sitcom, and the laugh track laughed a little too heartily at the lame jokes. Still, the sound filled up some of the silence. It would be more comforting to have Ben to talk it through with, but that wouldn't be fair to either of them. Firm boundaries were important in a situation like theirs. That's what everyone said, wasn't it? Boundaries were key. Why didn't boundaries feel like they were working?

Lord, take care of my father, she prayed for the hundredth time. The most frustrating part about her father was that he never appreciated how the women in his life worried. He never appreciated how they'd held his life together, either. Now he was sick, and he still wouldn't appreciate what she was doing here—or was that just his pride? She wished she knew.

Her cell phone rang, and Sofia snatched it up. It was Ben's number, and she felt a flood of relief. Maybe it wasn't wise to lean on him, but it might help her to calm her fears to hear his voice, too.

"Hi, Ben," she said.

"Hi, Sofia." There was a professional clip to his words that caught her attention. "How are you?"

"I'm fine." She wasn't, but that was the polite response. That was what people said when they were holding things together. Until everything crashed around a woman, she had the right to be most stubbornly "fine."

"I came across your father tonight."

So her father was with Ben. Or had been.

A wave of relief flooded over her. It helped to know, at least.

"Is he okay?" she asked.

"Oh, yeah, he's in one piece." She heard the irony in his tone.

"Good." She heaved a sigh. She didn't really need to know the details. "I was worried sick. I had no idea where he was. Where did you find him?"

"He was driving around town—"

"And he's on his way home?" she presumed. She wouldn't stand here, fuming in the kitchen. That was too much like her mother. She'd go upstairs and let him come back to a darkened home. She'd let him think that she'd gone to bed at her regular time—

"He was drinking and driving, Sofia."

She froze. "Drinking and driving? I don't believe that."

"I'm sorry." Ben sighed. "I pulled him over, and he had a lot of alcohol in his system. I brought him back to the station to sober up."

"I found out recently that he'd started drinking, but he promised me he'd stop. I didn't think that he'd go this far," she said feebly. "Obviously, he needs help. I'll see that he gets it."

This was the reason why she'd kept Jack away. This was the influence she wanted to avoid for her son. She'd stayed away for nine years in an effort to give her son something better, and here she was in the middle of her father's mess once again. Anger heaved up inside of her, but it was just as quickly engulfed in a tired sense of pity.

Sofia felt the tears rising in her eyes. It had been a long evening of worrying, and now all her worries seemed warranted. At least Ben had been the one to pull him over. If it had been another officer, it would be infinitely worse, she was sure. What her father needed was to get home, go to bed, sober up and be ready for his chemo treatment on Tuesday. What he needed was to get better.

"I'm glad it was you," she said, swallowing the lump in her throat. "Should I come get him, then?"

She'd have to wake up Jack, and that would ruin his sleep, and the poor boy would be a wreck for school the next day, not to mention all the confusion and questions. He'd never seen this sort of thing before, not in her raising of him. She'd protected him from this. Her childhood would not be repeated in her son's life.

"No," Ben said. "He's already sleeping it off."

"That might be better," she admitted, relieved that there was another way. She mentally recalibrated her plan. "I could come get him after Jack goes to school in the morning. It would spare Jack from seeing too much. I'm sure you agree that we don't want Jack to be affected by all of this—"

"Sofia, I've booked him. He's being charged with a DUI. After he's sobered up, he'll be let out on his own recognizance."

"What?" She felt as if the room had started to spin, and she reached out to plant a hand on the wall for balance. "Ben, you know how sick he is—"

"I know."

"And you know that he's just started cancer treatment. He's more frightened than he lets on about that."

"I know." His voice sounded low and sad. "This isn't the first time I've had to intervene when your father has been drinking. He's an alcoholic, Sofia."

"He drinks a little, but this is just the stress," she insisted, her own mother's words coming out of her mouth. Her mother had argued the same thing countless times, but... Could it be true?

"I've picked him up from the bar on many occasions and brought him home," Ben said. "I've pulled him out of bar fights. I've sobered him up after he spent days on end drinking in his house. That was his personal business. But drinking and driving is the end of the line."

Perhaps he did have a problem. She could concede to that. There were obviously things she didn't know about her father in those years apart, but that didn't mean that there wasn't a solution.

"Maybe he is an alcoholic," she said. "But he's my father, Ben, and I love him. I'll check him into a program, and I'll use my savings to pay for it. But you have to understand what he's been going through."

"I get it," Ben replied. "But, Sofia, he's already been booked. The charges are laid. He's going to have to see a judge over this."

Sofia blinked, the reality of the situation hitting home. Her father would go to court and get a criminal record. She knew how tough her father acted. She knew how "fun" he was for everyone else, but she also knew how frightened he was underneath that shell. He was a mess under there, and her father needed help.

"Please, Ben." She couldn't help the tremor in her voice. "Please, do something. He won't do this again. I'm sure he won't! Do this for me."

There was a pause—long enough that she could hear the muffled voices from the police station in the background. The sitcom from the other room laughed uproariously, and outside the steady drip of melting ice drummed out of rhythm.

"I'm sorry, Sofia," Ben said quietly. "I can't do it. I just wanted to let you know what was going on. I'll talk to you later, okay?"

Sofia didn't answer him; she simply hung up the phone. Standing there in the kitchen, she felt the weight of the world descend upon her shoulders. Ben had done it before—she'd watched him be lenient with that teenager, Ethan. She'd watched him just not lay charges, simple as that. If he could do it for Ethan, who was a troubled kid who hadn't been to school in months and was involved in drugs, why couldn't he do it for a fifty-eight-year-old cancer patient who'd made a bad choice? Why couldn't Ben do this for *her*?

She'd asked. She'd pleaded. He'd refused. The man who wrote his own rules was suddenly siding with the letter of the law. She'd never felt more betrayed in her life.

Ben looked down at his cell phone. She'd hung up on him. He sucked in a breath and looked in the direction of the drunk tank—a cell with some uncomfortable bunks used for the drunks to sober up. Steven was already snoring deeply. Normally the drunks weren't allowed blankets or pillows, mostly because they were hard to clean, but Ben had made an exception for Steve. When he finally woke up with a hangover as well as the chemo effects, he'd feel like misery personified, and a pillow might not be much, but it would be something.

Ben knew exactly what Sofia wanted him to do; he just couldn't do it. He couldn't bury this one, and not only because of the very real danger that drunk drivers posed to the community. Almost every year a high school student died from driving under the influence...or some innocent person who happened to be on the same stretch of road. Last year it was a teenage girl who was walking home from babysitting, hit by a drunk driver heading home from the bar. Driving under the influence was deadly.

But he wasn't only thinking about community safety. He was thinking about Steven, too. If Ben let Steven off this time, he'd be making things worse. Steven didn't need a pass right now; he needed a reality check.

Except Sofia couldn't see that.

Ben glanced at his watch. It was quarter past eleven, and way too late for a friendly visit, but he needed to talk to her. He couldn't have Sofia thinking that he was getting any kind of vindication out of this. He wanted her to understand. He *needed* her to understand.

He could stand here and argue with himself, or he could go down there and talk to her. He had no doubt that she'd still be up.

Ten minutes later, Ben pulled up in front of the McCray house and turned off the engine.

"Lord, give me the words," he prayed aloud.

He wasn't sure that words would make any difference, but he had to try. Ben got out of his car and made his way to the side door. He didn't want to wake up Jack, if he could help it. This was a discussion he needed to have with Sofia—alone.

When he got to the side door, he could see the light on in the kitchen. Sofia sat at the kitchen table, a tube of cookie dough on the table in front of her. She wasn't eating it, though. Her hair fell in disheveled waves around her shoulders, and she was staring straight ahead. He tapped on the glass, and she startled. When she saw him, the blank look turned to anger.

"What are you doing here?" she demanded as she opened the door.

"I felt like we needed to talk about this," he said.

"Do you, now?" She shook her head and walked back toward the table, but at least she'd left the door open. He stepped inside and closed it gently behind him.

"Are you okay?" he asked.

"No, I'm not," she retorted.

"I was afraid of that," he said. "I'm sorry... I really am."

"I want to know one thing, Ben. Why? Why won't you help us when you help everyone else?"

"It's more complicated than that," he said. He'd done what he felt in his gut to be right— and he was still convinced that it was right. If he'd taken the easiest route, he would have let Steve off the hook, but he hadn't.

"I don't see it!" Sofia's eyes glittered in anger, her cheeks flushed. "Ethan might be young, but he's a drug addict. My father is battling cancer, and you think he's less sympathetic?"

"Every human being deserves sympathy," Ben said, irritation beginning to simmer. "Do you think I have something against your father?"

"Don't you?" she demanded.

"No!" Ben attempted to find some inner calm. He moderated his tone. "I have nothing against your father."

"Not the fact that he hid Jack from you?"

She was lashing out, he could see that, but she had painful accuracy.

"*You* hid Jack from me." This wasn't exactly the direction he wanted the conversation to go, but she'd brought it up. "I don't blame your father for your choices, Sofia. You were an adult. You made a decision over and over again, every single day of Jack's life. So, no, I don't hold a grudge against your father."

She blinked, then swallowed hard. "So if your grudge is against me, why not help him, then?"

"Because it isn't good for him," Ben replied, his voice low and angry. "This isn't about sympathy. He's sick, and if he keeps drinking like this, he's going to die—either from the cancer, or from some horrific car accident. Do you think I'm just doing the easy thing here? The easy thing would have been to let him off, give him a warning. That would have been easy."

"It would have been *kind*." Tears welled in her

eyes, and she blinked them back. "That's what it would have been."

"No, it would have been irresponsible," he countered. "I have a responsibility to this community, as well as to your father. He doesn't need a break, he needs a reality check! Just because I love you—" He stopped, but the words had already left his lips.

"What?" Sofia froze and stared at him, her mouth slightly parted.

"Maybe I shouldn't have said that." He rubbed a hand over his eyes. In fact, maybe he should stop talking right now, but he was angry, and things were coming out. Maybe it was high time a few of these things were said aloud. "But I guess I've said it now. I do love you. I've loved you since we were teenagers, and that never stopped."

"You dumped me!" She turned her back on him and walked away, then came back, her eyes flashing. "How dare you say that you love me when you're the one who ended it?"

Could she really blame a seventeen-year-old for not understanding his feelings? He heaved a sigh. "I was scared. I wasn't graduating. I still had three classes to pass before I could get my diploma, but you were off on a scholarship. Your life was going on the way it was supposed to, and mine had stalled. I felt like a loser next to you!"

"And you blamed me?" she demanded.

"No!" He let out a frustrated breath. "I couldn't keep up with you! Your father was right. He told me that it was only a matter of time before you found some college guy and you forgot about me. I was leftovers from high school. I was a dumb kid, and my male pride told me that if I broke your heart first, it wouldn't hurt as badly when you found a guy who was better than me."

It didn't matter that he'd been asking for her hand in marriage at the time. It seemed so dumb now. If he'd been in Steve's shoes that day with his daughter's future on the line, he'd have done the same thing.

Sofia stared at him in silence. She opened her mouth as if to say something, then clamped it shut again. Her anger seemed to be melting away, and in its place, her chin trembled ever so slightly.

"Babe, I loved you." He stepped closer and put a hand out, running his fingers down her arm. "And, God forgive me, I still do."

Dare he tell her the burden he'd been carrying around with him all these years? He'd never spoken it aloud to anyone before, but the weight of it was crushing. He considered bottling it up and leaving it there, but the dam had been broken, and he found himself talking before he could think better of it.

"I loved you through every minute of my marriage to Lisa. She knew it, too. That's the worst part. She shouldn't have been insecure—she was amazing! But she was, because she knew that I still had feelings for a girl I'd fallen for years before I ever met her. You weren't puppy love, and Lisa knew the difference."

"You…" Sofia's voice was a breath. "But you loved your wife."

"I did." He nodded. "She was beautiful, sweet, smart… She was—" He swallowed a lump rising in his throat. "She wasn't you."

Sofia was so petite there in front of him, so warm, and she smelled so sweet. He moved a tendril of hair off her forehead and pressed his lips together, refusing to let himself make the mistake of kissing her again.

"I love you, too…" Her words were so soft that he almost didn't catch them. In fact, he wasn't even sure that she'd meant for him to hear.

"You do?"

Her words dug straight into his chest, and he wished he could cherish them there, but this was still wrong. She was still the woman whose memory had held him back from giving Lisa the devotion that was rightfully hers. Sofia might have loved him, but two people loving each other didn't make it right.

"But we can't do this," Sofia whispered.

"I know." He nodded slowly. "I need to get over you. Lisa and Mandy deserve that much."

Sofia reached up and put one hand in the center of his chest. He could feel the gentle pressure of her fingers touching his collarbone over the top of his flak jacket, and he put his hand over hers. Her skin was silky warmth beneath his rough fingers, and he wished that all of this could be different. He wished he'd been able to truly forget about Sofia during his marriage so that now this reunion wouldn't be so fraught with guilt.

"I might bend the rules sometimes," Ben said sadly, "but there is still right and wrong."

There was duty and there was penance. There were feelings and there were facts. His mother might weigh a heart more heavily than actions, but Ben didn't. His feelings didn't matter as much as the right thing.

"It's just as well." Sofia pulled her hand away and stepped back. "You broke up with me back then, and whatever the reason, you walked away. Having a child isn't reason enough to change that."

"Is loving each other reason enough?" he asked miserably.

"No." Tears rose in her eyes, and she shook her head. "I refuse to make my parents' mistake. They got married because my mother was pregnant with me. They loved as hard as they fought, from what my mother says, and in the end, they were miserable together." A tear escaped her lashes and trickled down her cheek.

"I'd never make you miserable on purpose," he said.

Even if they'd never be, she had to understand that. He'd never have made Lisa miserable on purpose, either, and he wasn't sure if he'd given her the happy life he'd promised her. Sometimes a man was better off on his own, where he couldn't disappoint and cause pain.

"No one means to—" She smiled sadly. "We all think we're doing what's best, and the end result is a mess. I thought I was doing what was best by hiding Jack from you, and you thought you were doing what was best by ending it back then. For what it's worth, I think you were right. It's better to end it sooner rather than later. I don't think I could survive a divorce—"

Tears choked her voice, and before he could stop himself, Ben wrapped his arms around her. She leaned into his embrace, her head resting against the crook in his neck. She smelled of floral shampoo and something unique that belonged only to her. He wished he could hold her here forever, never asking more of her, but he knew he couldn't.

"I've never loved anyone like I loved you," Ben said.

"Don't say that." She pulled out of his embrace and crossed her arms protectively over her chest. "Your life isn't over yet."

This was enough. Anything more, and he wouldn't leave. He needed to get out of there, to let the darkness outside swallow him up. This hurt more than he thought it would, and if he didn't keep moving, he'd do something he'd regret, like ask her to marry him. He walked resolutely to the door.

"Ben—"

Ben looked back, and Sofia wiped a tear off her cheek with the back of her hand.

"I wish it could be different," she said softly.

"Me, too."

He didn't trust himself to say anything more, so he pulled the door open and stepped outside into the chill of the night.

Give me strength, he prayed silently. The right choice was never the easy one. Ever. And tonight, the right choice left him empty and aching.

Chapter Fifteen

Sofia felt like a shell of her usual self as she helped her son get ready for school the next day. She attempted to smile, but by the time she sent him out to catch the bus, her face was tired from the mask. Nothing was heavier than a smile covering aching sadness.

She'd found a message on her cell phone that morning from an officer she didn't know telling her that her father was being released, but that a trial date had been set. They were aware of his chemo session and would transport him to the hospital so that he wouldn't be late. She could pick him up from there.

Her mother had been right about all of it. Her father was still too much to take care of on her own. And Ben was still too much like her father for her own comfort. She'd never realized that her dad was an alcoholic before. Did it change anything? Not really, but it did explain more about his inconsistencies. Maybe if he'd been dry, he would have been a better father. Maybe he'd have been a better husband, too, and her parents would still be together.

She glanced at her watch. She had one hour until her father's appointment, and she had a lot of things to discuss with him. She wouldn't lecture him. He was a grown man with an addiction, and she highly doubted that she'd be able to change something that her mother hadn't managed to make a dent in during their seventeen years of marriage. But she did have some questions she wanted answered. He was still her father, after all.

A lot had changed since last night. Her father had just stopped being the strong-willed rebel, too old for that leather jacket, and had turned into an alcoholic. Ben had changed from the boy who broke her heart into the grown man who'd broken her heart, except this time she couldn't blame him. She'd allowed herself to fall for him again, and while she'd denied loving him for as long as possible, that was the truth of it. She'd fallen in love with him all over again.

It didn't have a hope of working before—he'd just been a rebellious kid with a girlfriend, and she'd been the idiot who'd expected him to blossom into a husband and a life partner. It didn't have a hope of working now, either. He was now a widower with a heart full of guilt, and she was still the idiot who had allowed herself to hope—very deep down—that they might be something more, even though it was utterly impossible. Why couldn't she learn?

These same thoughts were swirling through her mind when, an hour later, she arrived at the hospital, parked and headed toward those double doors. Somehow, her feet were heavier, along with her heart. Had it been a mistake to drag Jack back to Haggerston? Should she have come out for a couple of weeks on her own and then gone back to California where everything was sunny and safe? But true to form, Sofia had dived in headfirst. She'd never been a halfway kind of woman, and it got her into trouble more often than not.

Sofia pulled open the door and came inside. The nurses nodded to her as she passed the desk and headed toward that semicircle of padded lounge chairs. Her father sat with his back to her, facing the window.

"Hi, Dad," she said softly, and her father startled. His PICC was already hooked up, and he had no reading material in his lap. Just him and his thoughts, it seemed.

"Hi, Sofia."

The pump churned softly beside his chair, and Sofia pulled up a chair of her own. "How are you feeling?" Sofia asked quietly.

"Like misery. I'm hungover." He lifted a bottle of water. "I'm supposed to drink even more of this to make sure I stay hydrated."

"Good idea."

Her father eyed her cautiously. "Are you still working with Ben?"

"No, our time is up. I've submitted my last article." She smiled wanly. "I'm taking over some local stories for another journalist who had a family emergency."

"Relieved to be done?" he asked cautiously.

She nodded. Relieved didn't actually cover it, but it would do. It would be better to get some space to let her heart heal. She'd written some solid articles that would inform the community about the kind of delicate work the police force was doing in this area. It would help give people a better idea of what the officers dealt with on a daily basis, and she hoped that they'd appreciate the sacrifice and service of the Haggerston officers. She hoped they'd understand some of the issues right next door...look out for each other a little bit more.

Her editor had been pleased with her work. Her assignment was completed...yet somehow, this still didn't feel over, at least not between her and Ben. But then, they were co-parents, so maybe it never would be.

"You're pretty mad at me, I guess," her father said.

"I was," she admitted. "Now I'm tired. And rather sad."

"I won't do it again," he said seriously. "I've never gotten behind the wheel while drunk before. I could have killed someone."

"You have a problem," she said softly.

"It looks like." His tone was gruff, and he looked away. "I always thought I could handle my liquor. You and your mom couldn't tell when I was drunk, and I thought that meant it was under control."

"That's not a good sign," she said.

"Maybe not." He sighed. "And I'm sorry. I know I always apologized, but I wasn't much of a dad to you."

That was true, and it was something he'd never admitted before. He'd always declared that she should be glad to have a dad, period. Lots of men just left. As if the bare minimum was something to celebrate.

"No, you weren't," she agreed. "I needed a father who would *be* a father. I didn't need a buddy, I needed a parent."

"I tried."

It didn't seem as if he'd tried much. Her father had never drawn any lines for her. He'd never forbidden anything. He was more interested in being her friend than helping her navigate her life with some boundaries and discipline.

"I did try," he said, when she didn't speak

for a moment. "You were a lot like your mom. You were more energetic, more high-tempered. You got mad easily and you cried easily. You got excited over these little things, and I didn't know—" He stopped and heaved a sigh. "I was a little afraid of you."

"That's silly, Dad," she said, smiling sadly.

He leaned his head back. "I did my best, though. I knew that you were a quality girl, and I made sure that your life would be better than ours was. That kid—Ben—I never actually forbade you from seeing him because I knew that I'd only make it worse. But I took care of things in my own way."

Sofia frowned. What had her father done behind the scenes exactly?

"How?" she asked.

"Well, the night before your prom, Benji Blake asked me if he could marry you."

His tone told her that he found the very idea ridiculous, and Sofia stared at her father in shock. Ben had wanted to marry her back then? This was news to her—she'd never realized.

"I told him in no uncertain terms that he wasn't good enough for you," her father went on, "and I told him that he'd never have my blessing. I might not have been as fatherly as I should have been, but I got the job done when it mattered. I made sure that he saw how things stood."

"And you told him that I'd go off to college and forget about him," Sofia concluded. "You told him that I'd meet some other guy who would be good enough, and I'd never think about him again."

"Something like that." Her father took a sip from his water bottle. "How did you know?"

She sighed. "He told me. That part at least."

"Anyway, I was looking out for you, baby girl." Her father's voice choked. "I wasn't going to let you end up with some kid with no future. You deserved better."

They sank into silence, but Sofia's mind was spinning. Ben had wanted to marry her…back then, before he felt any kind of pressure or responsibility toward her; he'd gone to her father in an old-fashioned gesture, and he'd asked for permission to marry her.

She wasn't completely sure what this meant, but it changed things. She'd been so afraid of reliving her parents' disastrous marriage, afraid of giving Ben cause to shout, "If it hadn't been for Jack…" Except that he'd wanted to marry her without even knowing of Jack's existence. Perhaps it was true back then, that Ben hadn't had much to offer. He hadn't even had potential, she realized wryly, but he'd managed to turn his life around. He'd worked to make this success for himself, and that was all due to God's grace and Ben's determination.

It was ironic that right now she'd be willing to take a chance on them again. Knowing this, having seen Ben's dedication to doing the right thing by his late wife, she wished that they could be something more and explore a little more deeply all these things they'd been trying so hard not to feel.

Except there still wasn't a way for it to work. It wasn't just her hesitation that stopped them; it was his sense of duty to his late wife. It was because of Sofia that he hadn't been able to be the kind of husband he wanted to be, and he'd never be able to forget that. No, her chance with Ben had passed, and he was right when he said that it was time to let go of whatever they'd had in the past and to move forward.

"Are you all right, Sofia?" her father asked, and she realized that her eyes had filled with tears. She blinked them back and nodded quickly.

"I'm fine," she said, her voice tight with sadness.

"You deserve better," her father repeated. "You're the best thing I ever managed in my life."

There had been a man she loved who wanted to be her husband without any arm-twisting or emotional gymnastics. He'd wanted to tie himself to her, and while they'd been too young to know what all of that meant, he'd kept on loving her as he grew up and made something honorable of himself, through the hills and valleys of the past nine years, and not at all because he knew about the child they'd made together. He'd wanted to marry her for *her*.

If there was a love better than that, she'd never heard of it. She realized that she and Ben would never be together, but she deeply hoped that she didn't deserve this for keeping their child a secret, because as a punishment, it was the worst she could imagine.

Ben came into the oncology ward, two cups of coffee in his hands. He wasn't even sure if Steve was allowed coffee during his chemotherapy treatment, but he hadn't wanted to come empty-handed. When he was informed that Steve had been brought here to wait for his daughter, Ben hadn't wanted Steve to sit alone.

That morning at the station, Mavis had come to see Mike. Mike would be facing criminal charges for domestic abuse, and he'd likely spend some time behind bars for this. He truly looked remorseful sitting in that cell with his head in his hands, but then every criminal did once they were caught. Mavis had told Ben that she was starting therapy. She had a lot to work through, and she didn't think she could handle it on her own anymore. Ben had never been more relieved. Getting help wasn't a sign of weakness;

it was a sign that she was ready to start fixing things, and Mavis deserved better than the life she'd been living. She deserved love and respect. She deserved to be safe.

The couple had sat in the visitor's room at the station, a pane of glass between them and phones at their ears. For the first time, Mavis had looked livid—and that was a good sign. Ben wished he could see the future for them. Would Mike get the help he needed to control his anger, or would this only harden him further? Would Mavis have the strength to stay away from him this time around? Or would the abusive cycle continue after Mike finished his time behind bars?

That was the hardest part of this job—all that gray area. There was right and there was wrong, and then there was that messy swath left behind it all...like the destructive path left by a tornado. How would the Laytons rebuild? That was up to them. A cop couldn't fix everything; he could only uphold the law and send up a prayer that God would do the rest. Ben could be here tomorrow, and the next day, and the next—he could keep showing up, and keep doing his job with as much heart and conviction as he could muster. He was doing it for the memory of Mandy, for Jack and all the other kids growing up in Haggerston—the kids who needed someone to count on when times got tough.

And he'd testify for the prosecution at Mike's trial. Nothing could hold him back from that.

It wasn't all about crime and punishment, though. He wasn't that inflexible. If only Sofia could see that. Whatever the cause, whatever the reason, they'd both been left with the fallout, and of all people, Ben understood why Steve had tried to drown his sorrows. Everyone else saw the jocular, happy Steve who was willing to lend a hand to a neighbor in need. Ben saw a different side to Sofia's father—the heartbroken man who lost the wife he didn't know how to keep, and the daughter he knew would resent him for it.

As he came up to the front desk at the oncology ward, he saw their backs—Sofia sitting next to her father—and he knew it was right. He hadn't been sure if Steve would be alone there or not, but she'd come to be with him, and that was the way it should be. Steve needed her. She needed her dad.

"Excuse me," Ben said quietly to the nurse at the station. "I just brought this coffee for those two over there—Steve and Sofia McCray. Would you mind giving it to them?"

She nodded, and Ben slipped away. He didn't want to be seen this morning. He and Sofia had said more than enough last night. They'd said it all, as a matter of fact, and there was nothing else to say. He loved her, even if he shouldn't.

She loved him, and they had no future together. If they were younger, he might have gotten a morose enjoyment out of the impossibility of it all, but he wasn't a kid anymore. All he could hope was that now that he'd taken the stand he should have taken years ago, God would heal his heart and help to make this easier.

His shoes echoed down the hospital hallway that led toward the main entrance, the emergency wing and the maternity ward. A stretcher rolled toward him, pushed by two ambulance medics, and Ben stepped into a hallway to let them pass. The stretcher rattled by with an old man hooked up to an IV. Ben stood motionless for a moment, and he glanced down the hallway he'd entered, realizing that it was the one that led to the maternity wing.

He knew better than to torment himself, and he hadn't been here since Lisa died, but he found himself walking back down that familiar hallway before he could decide better.

The maternity wing was slow that day, and he was grateful for it. He could hear the soft moans of a woman in labor farther down the hallway, and a heavily pregnant woman took tiny steps, one hand on her back, and her husband at her side. They didn't give him a second look, all their attention on the birth they awaited.

Ben understood that feeling—like the most important thing in the entire world was about to happen to them. He'd felt that with Lisa…and he wondered what Jack's birth had been like. Who had been with Sofia? Who had held Jack first? How big was he, and how had it felt to hold that squirming, healthy baby right after his appearance into the world? Who had grasped Sofia's hand and told her that she'd done a great job?

Mandy hadn't been squirming or healthy. She'd been sick and weak. She'd been too small to hold. He'd only been able to look at her through the clear walls of her incubator. Lisa hadn't been conscious for him to congratulate, and he'd been whisked out of the operating room so quickly that he still couldn't quite remember what had happened.

"Oh, Lisa…" Ben felt that familiar lump rise in his throat. He paused at the waiting room—empty at the moment—where he'd sat two years ago, waiting for news of his wife.

I'm sorry, he said in his heart. *I loved Sofia… I still did, but it didn't mean that I didn't love you, Lisa. I loved you, and losing you broke me. If I could have kept you with me, I would have—*

Somehow, he'd thought that if he kept his feelings a secret, he'd be able to fix them on his own, before Lisa was the wiser. He hadn't succeeded.

Ben sank into one of the hospital-issue chairs across from a little play station to entertain small children. Lisa wasn't there to hear his confessions or to absolve him. She wasn't there to forgive him and to take away his burden, but God was there. He could feel his Maker hovering close, and Ben wished he could just lean into his Father's arms and be held. Sometimes life hurt so much.

"I'm sorry," he whispered, and for a long moment, he just sat there, feeling the presence of God. Lisa wasn't here anymore, and even if he wanted to explain himself to her, he couldn't. He'd done his best as a husband, but being married hadn't been as easy as he'd thought it would be. Two very different people came together to live one life. There were bound to be rough patches, and if Lisa had lived, they'd have worked through every last one of them. When he'd married Lisa, he'd meant his vows: *'til death do us part.*

And death had parted them, leaving him on his own with all these memories and regrets.

There was a little church pamphlet lying on the seat next to him. Sometimes churches would leave brochures in places like this, hoping to encourage someone. He picked it up. This pamphlet was about heaven. A verse caught his eye:

"He will wipe every tear from their eyes. There will be no more death or mourning or crying or pain, for the old order of things has passed away."

He read the verse twice as the words sank

into his mind, and he felt the weight of his guilt lifting slowly from his shoulders. Lisa was with God now, and she was beyond tears and jealousies. She was most certainly beyond the pettiness of this world. If God had wiped her tears, then they were wiped indeed, and the young husband she left behind wouldn't be able to cause any more of them.

Lisa and Mandy were together, and they were in the safest place he knew: God's arms.

He sucked in a deep breath, and for the first time in a long time those tears that kept trying to push past his guard finally fell, and he silently wept for all that he'd lost. He cried for his wife and for his baby daughter, for the marriage cut short and for the ways he'd never been enough. He cried for the impossibility of it all— for the love he couldn't relinquish and the mistakes he'd made without ever having the time to right them. When he finally wiped his face and steadied himself, he felt lighter than he had in a long time. He might have loved Sofia still, deep in some corner of his heart, but he'd stood by his wedding vows, and he would have continued to do so. Thankfully God was the one who weighed hearts and motives, because he didn't trust himself to anyone else's judgment.

I still love Sofia, Lord, he prayed silently. *I loved her then and I love her now, and if things had turned out differently, I'd want a chance at a life with her...but they haven't. I trust myself to Your will. Please, Father, let my actions be pure. And I'll trust my heart to You.*

Chapter Sixteen

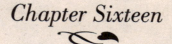

The next morning, Sofia stood at Ben's door, her purse hitched up on her shoulder and her heart hammering in her throat. She reached for the bell and listened to the echo of the chime inside. Maybe he wasn't even here... Was that what she wanted?

No, she wanted to sort this out. She wanted to find a balance that didn't hurt, where they could do what was best for Jack and at least know where they stood.

She also wanted to see him. Was that bad to admit? But she did. She longed to just look at him, and maybe explain the things she'd learned in the last day. She felt like she'd changed, and of all people, she wanted to tell Ben about it.

I am quite possibly the biggest glutton for punishment ever.

The door opened, and there stood Ben in a pair of jeans and a white tee that was sweaty around the neck, a towel in one hand. He was breathing hard and looked as if he'd been working out. He gestured her inside. The living room was tidy, except for a set of free weights sitting on the floor next to the couch.

"Is everything okay?" he asked, dropping the towel onto the floor next to the weights.

"It is." She nodded, then shrugged apologetically. "I just—"

She didn't know how to say it. Could she just blurt out that she missed him? Was that breaking all the silent rules of exes parenting together?

Ben's dark eyes met hers, and for a moment all that sadness and yearning passed between them unspoken. "Yeah, me, too."

Obviously their attraction wasn't going to go anywhere—not right away, at least.

Ben led the way into the kitchen, and he poured her a mug of coffee.

"I had a good talk with my dad yesterday," Sofia said. "He told me something I never knew before."

"Oh?" Ben poured himself another coffee and nudged the sugar in her direction. "What was that?"

"That you'd wanted to marry me." Her voice sounded strained when she said it, and she felt the heat rise in her cheeks. It wasn't a comfortable thing to blurt out like that, and Ben laughed softly.

"Yeah, I did. But your father was right. I wasn't old enough to be a husband. I didn't have much to offer."

"Still, it's nice to know." She smiled and put her attention into the bowl of sugar and coffee. "It means a lot to me, you know."

"If love had been enough to make a marriage work," Ben said, his voice low, "I would have had enough for both of us."

She smiled sadly. If only love were enough to conquer all the mountains between them, but she was willing to let her own desires go. She'd have to. If parenthood had taught her anything, it was that love wasn't about yourself, it was about the other person. Ben had been married before, and he couldn't just let go of his late wife so easily. Sofia had walked out of his life and he'd moved on. It was only fair.

"Just a minute," Ben said, and he left the kitchen.

Sofia stood alone, looking around. There were a few dirty dishes in the sink, and a large bowl held a huge bunch of green-tipped bananas on the counter. It felt strange to be in his kitchen by herself. A moment later Ben returned, something held between his fingers. He passed it over, and Sofia looked down at a ring with a tiny diamond chip in the center. She looked up at him in surprise.

"That's the ring I bought you all those years

ago," he said. "I asked your dad for your hand in marriage. That didn't go well." He smiled wryly. "I've held on to it all these years, and after some prayer and some thought last night, I think I'm finally ready to let it go."

"What do you mean...exactly?" she asked.

He stepped closer, and his dark eyes met hers with sadness. "I bought it for you, and I have to let go of these feelings somehow. I can't keep it any longer, and I wanted you to have it."

Sofia felt the tears well up in her eyes as she looked at that tiny ring. It wasn't worth much monetarily, but he'd sacrificed to buy it back then, and he'd done it for her. When she looked up, Ben touched the side of her face with the back of his finger, then he moved closer still and dipped his head down, catching her lips in his.

The kiss was lingering and sweet, filled with their mutual sadness. When he pulled back, she had to keep herself from moving into his arms. That would only make this harder.

"I'll be your friend, if that's what you want," Ben said quietly. "We're both Jack's parents, and I'll be a good dad. I won't let him down, or you, either, for that matter. I'll be good to you. You've already said where you stand, and I won't make you repeat it. I won't ask for more."

Sofia frowned, her mind spinning. Had he changed his mind about what he wanted? What was he trying to say? She shook her head.

"I thought that Lisa—"

"I've sorted a few things out," Ben said. "I've got to let go of my guilt, too. I did my best in our marriage, and I loved her. I would have been true to her if she'd lived, but she's not here anymore. And I don't need to protect her from anything. She's beyond pain and sadness. She's safe. But I know that I'm not what you want, and I keep telling myself I'll stop kissing you like that—" He shot her a rueful smile. "I won't pressure you."

"I've done some thinking of my own," she admitted. "I was terrified of ending up like my parents and having a man marry me because of the baby, not because he loved me. But you wanted to marry me without even knowing about Jack, and somehow you carried that love with you for nine years. That is nothing like my parents. Nothing. I should be so blessed."

Ben's obsidian eyes caught her gaze and held it.

"Are you saying you'd be willing to be something more?" Ben asked, unable to hide the eagerness in his voice.

This wasn't about games or winning or losing. This was about love, and about family. "Jack and I would be blessed to have you in our lives—" she smiled hesitantly "—as something more."

Without a word, Ben pulled her into his arms, and this time his kiss was unrestrained. He held her close, his strong arms twined around her waist as he kissed her, his lips moving slowly and thoroughly over hers, and when he had quite finished, he pulled back, looking down into her eyes.

"I was all-in then," he said quietly. "And I'm all-in now. Marry me, Sofia. Let's be a family."

Sofia nodded, tears rising in her eyes.

"Are you saying yes?" he asked, a smile flicking at the corners of his lips. "Because I've waited nine years for this, and I think I need to hear the actual words—"

"I will marry you, Ben, but one thing—"

"Anything." He still hadn't let go of her, and she had to wriggle her hand free, holding up the ring.

"I want this one." She looked down at the tiny diamond, the thin band... It was delicate and pretty, and it spoke of a tender love from all those years ago—something so fragile and impossible that had survived against all odds...

"That?" Ben shook his head. "Babe, I can afford a whole lot more than that now."

"I don't care." She met his gaze stubbornly. "I want this one—the one you bought for me back then when were young and idealistic."

Ben smiled, nodded, then slid the ring onto her finger. "Okay," he agreed. "But I choose the wedding band."

She laughed, blinking back tears. He'd choose

something that made up for the meager engagement ring, she was sure, but no matter how many diamonds glittered on that wedding band, it would never eclipse this one in her eyes.

"Is it really bad form to go get a kid out of class in order to tell him that his parents are getting married?" Ben asked. "I only ask because I'm kind of new to this…"

"How many times in a school year does that happen?" she asked, and then she laughed out loud at the sheer joy of it all. "Let's go tell him."

Ben pulled her close once more, kissing her lips, and releasing her to grab his keys.

"I love you, Sofia," he said softly.

"I love you, too, Benji." And as the reality of the situation fully registered, her heart soared in thankfulness. They were going to be a family. God had taken this mess of mistakes, and He had given them a second chance at forever.

* * * * *

Dear Reader,

I'm a mama bear kind of mom. I'm pretty sure I'm not alone in that! I'm protective and passionate. I take my job of mothering very seriously. It's my job to make sure that my boy grows up to be a good man, and I don't think that happens by accident. I want to raise a responsible, kind and hardworking man who can look back on his childhood and say, "She loved me like a rock."

I'm also aware that I'll have to let go one day, and there is this tiny worry in the back of my mind that a protective mama bear could turn into a bear of a mother-in-law! I don't think anyone means to overstep with their adult children, but I can see how easy it would be. You never stop loving your children, and you never stop wanting to protect them, either.

That personal worry is how this book was born. I wanted to look at both women in Ben's life—the girl who stole his heart and the mom who raised him. Making an alliance isn't always easy, and I think a lot of women can relate to that. But there is room in a man's heart for both his mom and his sweetheart, and when those women can be friends, they are absolutely unstoppable!

They say it takes a village, and I believe that. If it takes a village to raise a child, it also takes one to learn to let him go. It takes a village to support a marriage and to grow to be the mature, loving women we are destined to be. We *need* the village! It might not be easy, and it might not always be graceful, but no one said we had to do this alone.

If you'd like to connect with me, come find me on Facebook or on my blog at PatriciaJohns Romance.com. I love to hear from my readers, and you can count on a reply!

Patricia Johns

REQUEST YOUR FREE BOOKS!
2 FREE WHOLESOME ROMANCE NOVELS
IN LARGER PRINT
PLUS 2
FREE
MYSTERY GIFTS

✵✵✵✵✵✵✵✵✵✵✵✵✵✵✵✵✵✵✵✵✵✵

HEARTWARMING™
✾✾✾✾✾✾✾✾✾✾✾✾✾✾✾✾✾✾✾✾✾✾

Wholesome, tender romances

YES! Please send me 2 FREE Harlequin® Heartwarming Larger-Print novels and my 2 FREE mystery gifts (gifts worth about $10). After receiving them, if I don't wish to receive any more books, I can return the shipping statement marked "cancel." If I don't cancel, I will receive 4 brand-new larger-print novels every month and be billed just $5.24 per book in the U.S. or $5.99 per book in Canada. That's a savings of at least 19% off the cover price. It's quite a bargain! Shipping and handling is just 50¢ per book in the U.S. and 75¢ per book in Canada.* I understand that accepting the 2 free books and gifts places me under no obligation to buy anything. I can always return a shipment and cancel at any time. Even if I never buy another book, the two free books and gifts are mine to keep forever.

161/361 IDN GHX2

Name _____ (PLEASE PRINT)

Address _____ Apt. #

City _____ State/Prov. _____ Zip/Postal Code

Signature (if under 18, a parent or guardian must sign)

Mail to the **Reader Service:**
IN U.S.A.: P.O. Box 1867, Buffalo, NY 14240-1867
IN CANADA: P.O. Box 609, Fort Erie, Ontario L2A 5X3

* Terms and prices subject to change without notice. Prices do not include applicable taxes. Sales tax applicable in N.Y. Canadian residents will be charged applicable taxes. Offer not valid in Quebec. This offer is limited to one order per household. Not valid for current subscribers to Harlequin Heartwarming larger-print books. All orders subject to credit approval. Credit or debit balances in a customer's account(s) may be offset by any other outstanding balance owed by or to the customer. Please allow 4 to 6 weeks for delivery. Offer available while quantities last.

Your Privacy—The Reader Service is committed to protecting your privacy. Our Privacy Policy is available online at www.ReaderService.com or upon request from the Reader Service.

We make a portion of our mailing list available to reputable third parties that offer products we believe may interest you. If you prefer that we not exchange your name with third parties, or if you wish to clarify or modify your communication preferences, please visit us at www.ReaderService.com/consumerchoice or write to us at Reader Service Preference Service, P.O. Box 9062, Buffalo, NY 14240-9062. Include your complete name and address.

HW15

YES! Please send me **The Montana Mavericks Collection** in Larger Print. This collection begins with 3 FREE books and 2 FREE gifts (gifts valued at approx. $20.00 retail) in the first shipment, along with the other first 4 books from the collection! If I do not cancel, I will receive 8 monthly shipments until I have the entire 51-book Montana Mavericks collection. I will receive 2 or 3 FREE books in each shipment and I will pay just $4.99 US/ $5.89 CDN for each of the other four books in each shipment, plus $2.99 for shipping and handling per shipment.*If I decide to keep the entire collection, I'll have paid for only 32 books, because 19 books are FREE! I understand that accepting the 3 free books and gifts places me under no obligation to buy anything. I can always return a shipment and cancel at any time. My free books and gifts are mine to keep no matter what I decide.

263 HCN 2404   463 HCN 2404

Name	(PLEASE PRINT)	
Address		Apt. #
City	State/Prov.	Zip/Postal Code

Signature (if under 18, a parent or guardian must sign)

Mail to the **Reader Service**:
IN U.S.A.: P.O. Box 1867, Buffalo, NY 14240-1867
IN CANADA: P.O. Box 609, Fort Erie, Ontario L2A 5X3

READERSERVICE.COM

Manage your account online!

- Review your order history
- Manage your payments
- Update your address

> *We've designed the*
> *Reader Service website*
> *just for you.*

Enjoy all the features!

- Discover new series available to you, and read excerpts from any series.
- Respond to mailings and special monthly offers.
- Connect with favorite authors at the blog.
- Browse the Bonus Bucks catalog and online-only exculsives.
- Share your feedback.